SOUTH DAKOTA
Treaty Search

Books in the X-Country Adventure series

Message in Montana
South Dakota Treaty Search

SOUTH DAKOTA
Treaty Search

Bob Schaller

BakerBooks

A Division of Baker Book House Co
Grand Rapids, Michigan 49516

© 2000 by Bob Schaller

Published by Baker Books
a division of Baker Book House Company
P.O. Box 6287, Grand Rapids, MI 49516-6287

Printed in the United States of America

ISBN 0-8010-4451-0

Library of Congress Cataloging-in-Publication Data is on file at the Library of Congress, Washington, D.C.

While the things the Arlingtons learn about the history, culture, and people of the state are based on actual facts, their adventure itself is fictional.

For current information about all releases from Baker Book House, visit our web site:

http://www.bakerbooks.com

Contents

1 Mystery Unfolds   7
2 Tracking the Treaty   18
3 Meeting Jim Red Feather   28
4 Another Piece   37
5 The Safe-Deposit Box   44
6 The General's Letter   59
7 Behind the General's Eyes   71
8 The Puzzle Completed   80
9 Mitaku Oyasin   90

Fun Fact Files   97
Check It Out   107

Mystery Unfolds

"The Lakota warrior pressed the heels of his bare feet deep into the sides of his horse, supporting himself as he strung his bow and, with one swift, sure movement let the arrow fly.

"The Indian rode purposefully over to the fallen soldier. He rapped him on the back of the head with his bow as he passed by him on his horse, thereby 'counting coup.' The white man soon would die.

"But in his heart, Crazy Horse wanted only to serve the Great Spirit," the elderly Lakota woman said as she finished her story. "He wanted only to hunt the buffalo and roam the land. He wanted only to avoid genocide for his people and live apart from the white settlers, who crawled across the South Dakota prairie like ants as they rushed to the Black Hills—the 'Paha Sapa'—in their quest for gold."

Seventeen-year-old Ashley Arlington, her sixteen-year-old brother, Adam, and their parents, Alex and Anne, stood somberly with the other tourists at the base of the Crazy Horse Monument in the Black Hills of South Dakota. The sun beat down on the warrior's face, a magnificent eighty-eight feet, or nearly nine stories, from the top of the head to his chin.

The family had come from their home in Washington, D.C., to the Crazy Horse Monument for a special occasion. One weekend a year, visitors are invited to ascend to the top of the monument and see up close the face of a man held in the same regard by American Indians as the four presidents carved into Mount Rushmore—Washington, Jefferson, Roosevelt, and Lincoln—are by white Americans. Before the trip, Adam and Ashley had read about Crazy Horse and learned that the great leader of the Lakota people, also called the Sioux, was killed by Indian police and U.S. soldiers in 1877 at the age of thirty-five.

"How long until this monument is done?" Ashley asked the tour guide.

The elderly Lakota woman smiled sadly, shook her head, and said something in her native language that Ashley couldn't decipher.

Alex Arlington draped an arm across his daughter's shoulders as they began the trek up the monument.

"This monument probably won't be finished in my lifetime," he said. "Probably not even in yours," he added, running a hand through his thick, slightly graying hair.

"But, Dad, how long could it take?" Ashley asked, confusion showing in her blue eyes.

"Yeah, Dad," Adam chimed in. "They get a couple dozen rock drillers, and this thing could be done in no time."

The family had viewed the model at the base of the monument, a $\frac{1}{34}$ scale version of what the monument was to look like at completion, with Crazy Horse in a proud pose on his horse, leading his people into battle as his hair trails majestically in the wind.

Mr. Arlington sighed. "Well, the funding's limited. The family who is doing this—the sculptor Korczak Ziolkowski's widow and their ten children, who are sympathetic to what the Sioux were put through by the U.S. government—won't take federal funds. From what I understand, the government came in thirty years ago when this was just starting to take shape and offered to plunk down millions of dollars to get it done. The folks here at Crazy Horse said, 'Thanks, but no thanks.' They didn't trust the U.S. government to be involved in this, because the fact is, the government had never honored a single treaty with the American Indians."

"That's awful," Ashley said, absently tucking a lock of blond hair behind her ear. The family battled a stiff South Dakota breeze and rickety, suspended wooden steps as they hiked up the slope of the monument. "Really, they should just give in and get it done."

"Oh, I can't agree with you there, Ash," said her mother, Anne, a tall, athletic woman as blond as her two children. Mrs. Arlington was a part-time history professor at a college back home, and now her curly hair bobbed as she shook her head emphatically. "The Native American people have been lied to at every turn. Their land and homes and way of life were taken from them by force.

Can you imagine that, I mean, really imagine it? You can look at it one way, that we live in a world of conquerors, and the Indians weren't up to the challenge. But if you have a social conscience or don't like the thought of us getting kicked out of our houses someday just like what happened to the Indians, then you can see their perspective, can't you? And you can understand why they would want to handle this monument in their own time, their own way."

"I see what you mean, Mom," Ashley said after a moment, putting on the sweatshirt she had tied around her waist. "But I'd sure like to see the finished product."

"Well, at least we can respect what it stands for," Mr. Arlington observed. "And what it means to the Native American people. This is so much more than a rock sculpture. It's representative of a culture that is being lost. And that's a loss for all of us."

Now at the top of the mountain, the Arlingtons were dwarfed beneath Crazy Horse's commanding face. Looking around, they could see the rough-hewn rock below, rock from which eventually would emerge the warrior's torso and the horse that would bear him. Pamphlets in the visitors' center explained the history of the monument: It was begun by Korczak Ziolkowski. The Boston-born sculptor had received a letter from Sioux Indian Chief Henry Standing Bear, saying he longed for a monument to the American Indian. The chief had watched the carving of Mount Rushmore and wrote, "the Red Man has great heroes too."

Within a year of receiving Chief Standing Bear's invitation Ziolkowski had completed a clay model. In 1946 he came to the Black Hills, an area that covers fifty-six thousand square miles and has eighteen peaks of at least seven thousand feet, and set his sights on the six-hundred-foot mountain that would become his canvas. Ziolkowski decided to use the whole mountain for his tribute to the great Sioux warrior, Crazy Horse.

"So, what do you say, Ashley?" Adam asked as he stood face to chin with Crazy Horse. "Do you think Crazy Horse would like this monument?"

"I'm not sure," Ashley said. She was quiet for a moment, looking around at the tourists who'd also made the climb to view Crazy Horse close up. "But it says something anyway that we're all here together today," she said at last. "White people, African Americans, Indians, Asians—we're all here, united and peaceful, no matter what awful things happened in the past. It doesn't do Crazy Horse and his people any good. But at least it's something."

The family made good time hiking down the monument. Adam, a standout on the cross-country team at Thomas Jefferson High School and a skinny five-foot-nine, was always ready to speed up the pace. And Ashley, who'd been elected co-captain of the next season's basketball team, gave her brother some healthy competition, jogging back down the slope. Soon they were down the hill and inside the gift shop at the base of the Crazy Horse Monument.

The time the Arlingtons had planned to spend at Crazy Horse was starting to run out as Ashley and Adam went through the various books, T-shirts, and other souvenirs. The family's motor home was lodged comfortably in the prairie of Wind Cave National Park, just a short drive from Crazy Horse Monument near the town of Hot Springs.

Wind Cave was an experience that could last several days in itself, and so far the Arlingtons had explored only a fraction of the seventy-nine known miles of underground passages and almost thirty thousand acres of above-ground wilderness and wildlife.

Tonight was to be special for Alex and Anne Arlington. They were going to have a night out together checking out the sights and sounds of Deadwood, an area in the Black Hills famous for the likes of Wild Bill Hickok and Calamity Jane. An evening alone with Adam and his computer looming ahead of her, Ashley was eager to buy a good book about Crazy Horse before they left the gift shop. She settled on one by long-time Crazy Horse biographer Mari Sandoz. Ashley reached to the back of the stack and pulled the copy that was second from the back—a particular book-buying quirk of hers.

The six books looked much older than the other Crazy Horse books in the shop, many of which had the same title but different colored covers. The one Ashley had chosen was printed in 1942 and was in good shape for being an original. Still, she could've saved forty dollars by buying one of the sharper looking 1994 reprints.

"Mom, is it okay if I get this one?" she asked, showing her mom the price.

"Sure, Ashley," her mother answered. "It's your baby-sitting money, so it's up to you."

Ashley took the book to the cash register and pulled out her wallet. "Sweetie, you are so lucky," the clerk said with a broad smile. She was an older lady with coarse, graying hair and deep creases around her smiling eyes. "These books are a sort of treasure," she added.

She then leaned across the counter as if to share a wonderful secret. "One of the elders from the Pine Ridge Indian Reservation got a box of those books when they were printed way, way back. Anyway, this man died in 1945, and his family boxed up his belongings and left them in a garage on the reservation.

"His granddaughter—she's also a Sioux of course—brought them in just today for us to sell. You know, for the monument," the lady said, nodding her head. She put the book in a sack and handed it to Ashley. "Enjoy it."

"Yes, ma'am," Ashley said, as the lady smiled glowingly at her.

Ashley's father caught the tail end of the clerk's words and asked what it was all about.

"Dad, this book is like fifty years old," Ashley said proudly. "Fifty bucks is a lot of money, but I got a piece of history."

"Hey!" Adam hollered to his sister that night after their parents had left for Deadwood. "You won't believe this!"

Ashley was washing her face in the bathroom of the forty-foot motor home. She stepped out and saw the hookup leading from the cell phone to Adam's computer. He was researching online, his favorite pastime.

"Ashley, check this out," Adam said, his brown eyes bright. "Look, here's Sturgis, just twenty-one miles up I-90 from Rapid City. A small town, right?"

Ashley shrugged. "If you say so."

"About six thousand residents," Adam said. "But it says here that more than one hundred thousand bikers head to Sturgis each year for a Harley-Davidson convention. Can you believe that?"

"Vroom-vroom," Ashley said, tugging gently at the back of Adam's blond hair as he looked up and grinned. She smiled at her brother and grabbed a battery-powered camping lamp to take outside.

Ashley set the lamp on the picnic table and unfolded a comfortable lawn chair. She pulled mosquito netting down on the sides of the awning of the motor home. Sitting in the brisk air beneath the canopy of the dark South Dakota sky, a Native American quilt her mom had bought that day wrapped around her legs, Ashley opened her new book. The pages were yellow and stiff but in good condition. Ashley was tantalized immediately, reading about the very prairie on which she had walked that day. The book got right into the Indians' relationship with buffalo, and the family had seen lots of buffalo around Wind Cave.

Ashley read for quite a while, dozed, and read some more, closing in on page one hundred of the 340-page book. *Mom and Dad should be home soon,* she thought as she peeked inside the camper and saw Adam sleeping. The clock read 12:15 A.M., so she decided that she too should call it a night. The book wasn't going anywhere—Crazy Horse would be there in the morning, counting coup and giving ponies to those in his tribe who were needy or had none.

Flipping through the pages she'd read, Ashley felt the book's heft. She turned to the last page of the book to see how many pages were left to read. Noticing a break in the pages, Ashley gently held the book by its binding and slowly shook it back and forth. A piece of badly worn paper, not even four inches wide by five inches high, folded in half, fell out and drifted to the ground. It was much thicker than the pages of the book.

Ashley picked it up and held it closer to the light to get a better look. The lines were broken and no sentence was finished.

On this 1st day of January, 18__
America and all American Indians agree
which is binding here in this form, and wi__
days. This treaty finalizes all arrangement__
and land rights to the Black Hills in th__
until a time 11 years from now on the first a__
Nation is to assume full control of the Bl__
all land rights to the Black Hills. As o__
allowed in the Black Hills. All rail lin__
government, and all roads will be left to __
see fit.

General George Crook

Captain William Grattan

Chon-gah-ma-he-to-haas-

Wah-ke-ke-yan

Ma__

Quietly, she read each line: "On this 1st day of January, 1875 . . . America and all American Indians agree . . . which is binding here in this form, and will . . . days. This treaty finalizes all arrangements . . . and land rights to the Black Hills in the . . . until a time 10 years from now on the first . . . Nation is to assume full control of the Bla— . . . all land rights to the Black Hills. As of . . . allowed in the Black Hills. All rail lines . . . government, and all roads will be left to . . . see fit."

Unable to make sense of the fragmented writing, Ashley studied the first two hand-scrawled signatures below it. One was General C-something, but she couldn't make out the rest. The other signature was something *Gratton*. Below those were what looked like three signatures in a language that made no sense to Ashley. But what was this paper? Whose were the signatures? And where could the rest of the thing be? In the Black Hills somewhere? Maybe back home in Washington, D.C., with other U.S. government documents?

"Adam!" Ashley called, quickly hopping the stairs into the motor home.

Shaking off the deep sleep he had been enjoying only for an hour, Adam sat up and yawned. Ashley showed him the paper and breathlessly told him how it had fallen out of the book.

Adam yawned again.

"Quit yawning, this is exciting!" his sister shouted.

Just then, their parents pulled into the campground.

"Good! Maybe Mom and Dad will be awake enough to appreciate this!" Ashley said indignantly. Adam flopped back down on his bed.

Ashley showed the paper to her father and mother as soon as they came up the steps.

"What do you think it is?" Ashley asked.

"I don't know," her father answered. "Any thoughts, Anne?" Mr. Arlington gently placed the paper in the palm of his flat hand, sensing its brittleness.

"I don't know for sure," she said. She put on her glasses and guided her husband's hand under a light for a better look. "But if I had to guess, I'd say it looks like it might be part of a treaty."

A treaty! Ashley and Adam looked at each other in amazement. If it was signed according to the day in the lower left-hand corner, the document was 122 years old.

Ashley told the whole family what the clerk at the souvenir shop at Crazy Horse Monument had told her, about how a Sioux elder had bought the books from their original printing more than half a century ago.

"Were there other copies of the book at the shop?" Mrs. Arlington asked, her blond curls bobbing.

"Five in the store, plus this one," Ashley recalled, holding up her copy of the book.

Mr. Arlington smiled, a sparkle in his brown eyes. "As usual, our vacation is turning out to be very intriguing," he said. "Let's head back to the monument in the morning, first thing. We'll see if there are any more pieces to this puzzle."

Tracking the Treaty

The family piled into the car early the next morning and pulled through the gates of Crazy Horse Monument just as workers were opening up for the day.

As everybody climbed out of the car, Ashley looked up at the face of Crazy Horse carved into the hill.

"Boy, what I wouldn't give to be able to ask him just a couple of questions," she said.

"That might clear up a few things," her father said with a smile. "Speaking of which—hold on, gang, and come here for a second."

Ashley, Adam, and their mother huddled around Mr. Arlington, warming each other in the chilly morning air. A strong wind was blowing, and everyone was bundled up in sweatshirts or hooded windbreakers.

"We need to make a big decision here," Mr. Arlington said, his attorney's mind clicking into gear. "If we show this to the people in the shop, they might decide that it belongs to them—and that certainly is a possibility. Or we could go to a museum or library and see what we could find. Or, we could just go to the local sheriff or district attorney's office and . . ."

"And what, Dad? Turn it over to the government?" Ashley asked with a look of disbelief. After reading about Crazy Horse, she was caught up in the plight of the American Indians, more aware than ever of the misdeeds of the past.

"Okay, Ash, take it easy. Let's poke around and find out what we can," her mother said, putting a calming hand on her daughter's shoulder as the four headed into the gift shop.

After gently leafing through the pages of the other five books, the Arlingtons looked around some more. They asked a clerk, an elderly woman but not the same one from the day before, if there were any books about the history of treaties.

"Most all of the books here have some information on just about all of the treaties," the woman said. "But one with all the treaties listed? Not that I know of. You'd be more likely to find something like that at the public library in Rapid City."

Adam tapped his mother's shoulder.

"Mom, I could track down some of this when I plug in my computer today," he said. Mrs. Arlington nodded in agreement. The family picked out some more gifts—matching coffee cups for Mr. and Mrs. Arlington and T-shirts with a screening of the Crazy Horse Monument for Ashley and Adam—and brought them up to the counter.

The clerk rang up the items. "You know," she began, "a descendant of General Crook is speaking over at Mount Rushmore today. If you're interested in that sort of thing, you might like to hear what he has to say."

"I don't understand," Mr. Arlington said. "Was this General Crook a treaty writer?"

"No," the woman answered. "But the people believe he had an honest heart, and he was the only white man that the Indians back in the 1870s could trust to keep his word."

"We were headed to Mount Rushmore today anyway," Mr. Arlington said to Ashley as they walked back out to the parking lot. "This could be even more worth our while."

The family drove through the towns of Custer and Hill City before stopping in Keystone to buy some postcards. Adam had downloaded a couple of files from the Internet, and he was scanning his screen as they drove, something his mother didn't like. "You'll miss the scenery for studying the map, Adam," she'd often say. But now, Adam and Ashley were talking about the route they had taken to Keystone.

"Look at this, Ash. Custer State Park is huge, I mean really huge," Adam said, pointing just south of Mount Rushmore on the map on his computer screen. "And look over here. By Flintstones Bedrock City and the National Museum of Woodcarving, there's that city we passed through, Custer. I mean, General Custer has a big ol' state park—seventy-three thousand acres—and a city named after him. And all Crazy Horse gets is an unfinished rock."

"That doesn't seem fair," Ashley agreed. "You know, I almost wish Custer and Crazy Horse and the other leaders from both sides during that time could come back and talk about how it really was. There are two such different recordings of the history from that era. I mean, sure, I know the truth lies in the middle, like Dad always says. But where's the middle ground on this one?"

Keystone was only a couple of minutes from Mount Rushmore. As the family turned a corner up the hill to Mount Rushmore, the presidents' four faces, perched nearly fifty-five hundred feet above sea level, finally came into sight for the first time. The family let out a collective gasp at the magnificence of the view. The presidents' heads were so big that each man would stand 465 feet tall if the whole body had been sculpted in addition to the heads. That means each head is as tall as a six-story building.

"It's even more breathtaking than I ever could have imagined," Mrs. Arlington said.

"Yeah, I had only seen it in a cartoon, except for the picture I saw on that national parks CD-ROM," Adam added.

The family parked in the spacious parking lot and walked toward the faces of the presidents. The sidewalk under the recently renovated grounds at Mount Rushmore had a long walkway lined with flags from all fifty states. At the visitor center, the Arlingtons viewed a video that explained how sculptor Gutzon Borglum crafted his plans to carve a national monument into a mountain. With its completion in 1941, Mount Rushmore quickly became a big part of America, generating a sense of patriotism not unlike the American flag or the Statue of Liberty.

The Arlingtons stopped in a gift shop for some fudge before settling in to hear Elijah Benjamin Crook, the great-great-grandson of General George Crook.

Dressed in black jeans and a black leather vest over a long-sleeved shirt, Elijah Crook spoke for well over an hour. He was sympathetic to the cause of the American Indian and was careful to address the prevailing sentiments of the time during which his great-great-grandfather lived. There was no question that he was proud of General Crook. The members of the audience could hear the affection in his voice as he spoke about how dignified his great-great-grandfather looked in a portrait housed in Elijah Crook's home.

"That portrait was done not far from here," Elijah Crook said. "Just a handful of miles south of the Black Hills."

After he finished speaking, Mr. Crook took questions from the audience. Most of the people wanted graphic descriptions of the battles his ancestor had fought. But he apparently wasn't interested in discussing lines of battle and bloodshed. Instead, he quoted his great-great-grandfather's famous line spoken when asked about the difficulty of fighting the Indians: "Yes, it is hard. But, sir, the hardest thing is to go and fight those whom you know are in the right."

A young woman in the audience wearing a University of California at Berkeley sweatshirt stood to ask a question. "How come the government kept signing treaties and then breaking them?"

"That is perhaps the best question of all," Mr. Crook said. He shook his head slowly. "There is no real answer to it. After all the treaties were broken, there's some evidence from a letter my great-great-grandpa sent back to a commanding general in Washington that another treaty was written, signed, and all set to be enforced. But an

Indian tore it into four pieces, and he and his other Indian leaders stormed out of a soldiers' fort near here in the Black Hills."

The Arlingtons looked at each other.

"The treaty, Dad!" Ashley said to her father.

"Mr. Crook," Mrs. Arlington called out, waving a hand. "Any idea what year that treaty, the one that was torn up, was signed before it was destroyed?"

"I'd have to check with family files back in Washington, D.C.," he said. "But if I recall correctly, General Crook's letter was dated sometime late in 1875."

"And do you have any idea what the treaty was about?" Mrs. Arlington pressed.

Elijah Crook took a long, hard look at Mrs. Arlington and her family. "No, ma'am, I really don't," he said after a moment. "And I don't recall the letter being very specific about it either," he added. "It's actually quite the source of confusion for us to this day. My great-great-grandfather wrote in the letter that the answer could be found 'Deep in my eyes.' No one has ever understood what he meant by that. We briefly entertained the notion of even exhuming his body. But with no more information to go on than that, we couldn't justify disturbing the general's final resting place. It's just been the one mystery we've never found a key to unlock, but I sure appreciate your interest."

The Arlingtons stared at each other in amazement.

"We are onto something for sure," Ashley whispered excitedly to her brother.

After the program was over, the Arlingtons returned to the gift shop, hoping to have a chance to speak with Elijah Crook privately. But by the time the slowly milling crowd let them through, he was gone.

The next stop was Rapid City. The Arlingtons decided to take a peek at Native American books in the public library.

Ashley found some interesting facts in a book about the Black Hills and the whites' quest for gold there. The Indians had, at one point, agreed to sell access to the Black Hills to the white men. However, the only Indians who signed the treaty were not chiefs or even really leaders of their respective tribes.

Ashley quietly approached a library clerk who was stacking books from a rolling cart.

"Excuse me," Ashley said to him. "I am—well, my family and I, we're looking for information on treaties between the Indians and the U.S. government."

"Over there is a whole section of books on Native Americans," the man said. "I don't know that any are specific enough to define all the treaties, but I'm sure they mention a fair number of them."

"We've been looking through those already—those are my parents over there right now," Ashley said.

Adam came walking up to the discussion at that point and asked if the library had Internet access. The clerk pointed him to a table near the reference desk, and Adam set up his computer. He popped in a disk in case he wanted to copy any of the information he found.

Going into a search mode, Adam looked for information on treaties. Having little luck with that, he scanned for information on American Indians in South Dakota. He called up some information on Crazy Horse and then scanned through the various Indian reservations in South Dakota.

"Look at this, Dad," Adam said, quietly waving his father over. "There are so many reservations around here—in the western part of the state is the Standing Rock Indian Reservation. That one extends into North Dakota. Just below that one is the Cheyenne River Indian Reservation, see? And then north of Trail City is where Sitting Bull's grave is, in the Standing Rock Reservation. That's right outside Mobridge."

Mr. Arlington nodded. "You know, Sitting Bull had quite a bit of power within the Sioux, I understand. He was a more 'official' figure for the Sioux, whereas Crazy Horse was more of a natural leader, one who didn't have the title of chief but was pretty much regarded as one among his people."

Mr. Arlington pointed at a web page on the computer screen. "This is a place we should check out," he said. The page showed an area of southern South Dakota near the Nebraska border called the Pine Ridge Indian Reservation.

"It says it's home to much of the Badlands National Park. Wounded Knee is there too—where the infamous massacre took place."

The library clerk shelving books nearby spoke then. "You know something," he said, "there's a man who gives tours down at the Badlands. I don't know if he could answer all of your questions, but he could definitely do better than I have."

Ashley smiled at the man.

"He's Indian," the clerk continued, sliding another book onto a shelf. "He has some standing among the Lakota, although I don't know if he is as active now as when I first heard about him."

"When did you first hear about him?" Ashley asked.

"Oh, back in high school, so about twelve years ago," the clerk said. "I'm from here, so I've been to all the parks and attractions several times. Anyway, this guy might be able to help you."

"Do you know his name?" Ashley asked.

"I know he's a Red Feather, but I don't know his first name," the man said. "You'll have to get a little lucky to find him. But if you ask for an elder named Red Feather down there at Badlands National Park, you should have a shot at finding him."

"Okay," Ashley said. "Thanks a lot for your time."

"You bet," the man said. "I hope you find what you're looking for."

The family was soon driving east of the pine-forested Black Hills on State Highway 44 southeast toward Scenic, an appropriately named town just off the west end of the sprawling Badlands National Park. Ashley had briefed her mother on what the man at the library had said. Her parents, who planned a trip to the Badlands anyway, were more than happy that the quest had led them there.

In Scenic, the family stopped to get soft drinks and juice. Ashley and her father talked to the woman working behind the counter at the convenience store.

"Oh, yes," the woman replied. "Everyone knows who the Red Feathers are. But you're still a good way from there. They're on the east side of the park, near the Prairie Homestead area."

The family toured the Badlands as they made their way closer to where Red Feather was supposed to be. The Badlands were spectacular, providing a savage landscape of deep gorges and lunarlike spires of bizarre pinnacles and massive buttes carved by the wind and rain over the centuries.

"The Red Feathers?" a Native American said when they stopped at another convenience store. "Sure; go about six miles up the road, and you'll see a set of four gray houses on the right side of the road. You're probably looking for Jim Red Feather; his house has the red barn in back."

"Thanks," Ashley said, as her father paid for two bottles of water.

"Or," the man said, leaning over the counter and peering out the window to the parking lot, "you could go out front to pump three."

Meeting Jim Red Feather

Jim Red Feather had just pulled in and was filling his rusty, blue pickup with gas. "Looks like he's got his daughter's girls with him," the store clerk added as Ashley pulled her father out of the store and across the first set of pumps. Adam and his mother were already in the SUV, parked against the curb in front of the store. Wondering what was going on, they jumped out of the car and followed.

"Mr. Red Feather?" Ashley asked, smiling as the man paused, washing his windshield.

"I am Jim Red Feather." He was about an inch shorter than the 5′10″ Ashley and wore jeans and boots and a brown leather vest over a long-sleeved, button-up shirt. His black and gray hair was pulled firmly back in a ponytail. The lines in his face yanked toward his ears as he squinted at the Arlingtons.

Jim Red Feather nodded when Ashley introduced herself and her family, but he didn't seem eager to engage in conversation. "Are you looking for something?" he asked. The two young women in the pickup looked out. Both had long black hair and dark, inquisitive eyes.

"Well, sort of, Mr. Red Feather," Ashley said. "This is such a long story, and I feel bad bothering you like this, but it seems really important and might even be more important than that."

The man seemed to drop his guard in the face of Ashley's earnestness. "Tell me, child," he said softly.

Ashley took a deep breath. "Well, we were at the Crazy Horse Monument, and there were these books brought in that belonged to a Sioux elder," she said.

"Who was the Sioux elder? I am sure I would know him," he said.

"That's the thing; the books were brought in by a young woman because the Sioux elder had died," Ashley explained. "Anyway, these books are like fifty years old. And in the back of one of the books there was this piece of paper."

Mr. Arlington pulled out a copy of the treaty that he had photocopied at the library, keeping the original safe in the glove compartment of the SUV. Jim Red Feather took the paper Mr. Arlington offered and looked down at it for a long moment.

"Who would have thought . . ." he said quietly.

"Who would have thought what, Mr. Red Feather?" Ashley asked.

The soft-spoken man continued to stare at the paper, transfixed. "The rest of it—do you have it or do you know where any of it is?" he asked.

"We don't," Ashley said. "And I'm sorry. But, Mr. Red Feather, does this mean anything to you?"

"Does this mean anything to me . . ." he repeated softly, his eyes still fixed on the paper. He looked up at Ashley and then glanced inside the truck at his granddaughters. "You want to know if this means anything to me," he said, as his granddaughters climbed out of the truck to stand beside him.

Ashley felt her throat go dry. She was suddenly a world away from their life back in Washington, D.C., and every moment stretched as she waited for Jim Red Feather to speak.

"Yes, this paper means something to me," he said finally.

The wind had momentarily dissipated as the seven people stood under the clear South Dakota sky. A big-rig truck had rumbled past on the small state highway a few minutes earlier, but there was not a noise to be heard as the wind died down.

"My uncle and my father once told me of this," Red Feather said. "We did not talk about it much after that. I remember I was maybe sixteen years old, just became a man, so it was almost fifty years ago when I first heard about it. I heard about it again, once, in 1973." He stopped speaking again, as if lost in thought.

"Mr. Red Feather?" Ashley said quietly.

He looked up again, focused on her face. "I do not know where to start," he said. "I do not know what I should say."

Just about anything would have worked for Ashley and her family at that point.

"Are you in a hurry?" Jim Red Feather asked the Arlingtons.

"Not really," Mr. Arlington said. "We're on vacation."

"Could you join us, my family and me, for a couple of hours?" he asked. "These are my granddaughters, Robin and Denise," he added, pointing to the young women standing beside him. "We are headed to meet with several relatives at Wounded Knee. We will have a meal and talk there."

Mr. and Mrs. Arlington agreed they'd follow Jim Red Feather. As they started to walk back to their vehicle, he held Ashley in a long look. "You need to know about this paper," he said. "And I need to share it with my family," he added, placing a hand on a shoulder of each of his granddaughters.

"Is it important?" Ashley asked.

"Yes—it is important. This paper supposedly had the terms of a treaty on it. If it had not been torn up, if it had become the law of the land . . ." His voice fell away.

"What I am saying to you, to my granddaughters, is that this piece of paper could have changed the fate of white people and Indian people forever. We never were really sure what this treaty said. We could only go by what had been passed down through the years, some of which was never retold and some of which might have had some embellishment. From what I understand though, roads could have been overgrown with prairie. The whites could have had their precious gold, and we could have still led our lives our own way. That is just what I heard. I have always wanted to see the entire document to find out exactly what it said."

Jim Red Feather seemed to shake himself out of a reverie. "But we will talk more later," he said.

The Arlingtons sat in the car while Jim Red Feather paid for his gas. A million thoughts raced through their heads, yet no one said a word. The silence was broken by his footsteps. He pressed his lips together in neither a smile nor a frown as he passed the Arlingtons' vehicle on the way to his truck.

He hadn't said much. And while his words only raised more questions, he did answer the question of whether the document had any real significance.

And that answer, clearly, was yes.

The two vehicles turned south on State Highway 44 across flat landscape. Clouds first threatened, then burst into a brief, violent thunderstorm. The windshield wipers struggled to keep the glass clear, but the storm soon passed on. The Arlingtons followed the old blue pickup onto a small county road, heading southwest until the two vehicles reached Kyle, a town within the Pine Ridge Reservation. They saw a few houses, small and tired-looking, and a weather-beaten storefront. They drove on.

Wounded Knee was just a few miles from the eastern border of the reservation. It was hard to believe that anything could capture the Arlingtons' attention, so focused were they on the treaty. But as they got out of their car and walked through the plain archway into a wide, grassy area, they were transported back to 1890 when the Massacre at Wounded Knee took place. Jim Red Feather introduced the Arlingtons to his family and then began a remembrance of Wounded Knee.

He told of a Lakota man named Wavoka and the religious movement he started, the Ghost Dance, meant to unite Indian people with their friends in the ghost world.

"As the movement spread from tribe to tribe, the Ghost Dance took on a broader meaning, a meaning Wavoka never intended," Jim Red Feather explained. "Tribes began dancing and singing to make the world open up and swallow up all other people, leaving Indians alone on the land, a world returned to the beauty and peace it had enjoyed before white settlers came and ripped it apart searching for gold."

Pausing, he looked over at Robin and Denise. "Do you remember your grandmother and I telling you this story?" he asked them.

"Yes, Grandfather," they replied, almost simultaneously. "We miss hearing her voice," Robin added. Their grandfather was silent for a moment; then he continued.

"In 1889, the Lakota sent a group to meet with Wavoka. This group brought the dance back to the reservation and made sacred shirts in preparation for the Ghost Dance. So feverish was the belief in the Ghost Dance that the shirts were believed to be bullet-proof." He stopped and looked around at the grassy field, his eyes taking in the tobacco and eagle feather offerings left there for the people long-dead. The other Native Americans were nodding and shaking their heads, knowing the end of the story.

"The Ghost Dance caught on so, took such hold on the Lakota, that the people were united in a powerful way. White settlers were frightened. So frightened that in 1890, the U.S. Army killed more than two hundred Lakota people, mostly women and children and old people. Killed them right here where we are sitting. And we remember them today."

Adam and Ashley felt uncomfortable, hearing the story. Jim went on to tell of the seventy-one-day occupation of Wounded Knee by the American Indian Movement in 1973, an action taken to protest against the reservation's officially sanctioned government. Nearly twelve hundred were arrested, and two people were killed.

Jim Red Feather looked up and pressed his lips together.

"But we have moved on. At the same time that we must never forget these things, we must also put them behind us, for our own survival." He opened his arms wide, as if to join the silent group in an embrace. "*Mitaku Oyasin,* it is said—'we are all related.'"

Nearly two hours passed as stories were told. Then Jim Red Feather stood and addressed the sixteen people, all of whom were sitting, eating, except for one woman, who was tending to the cooking fire. The sun was angling low in the sky behind a few clouds as Jim spoke about the piece of paper Alex Arlington had given him that afternoon.

Only two of the other Indians were elders; three were children, plus Robin and Denise. Four were adults about the same age as Mr. and Mrs. Arlington, in addition to Jim Red Feather. All were part of the Red Feather clan, directly or indirectly. One of the men was Jim's brother Tom, and another, Leonard Jumping Bear, was a brother-in-law of Jim and Tom. Leonard's wife, however, had passed away years earlier, and he was without other family on the reservation. Leonard's family had been fragmented over the years, and not many even visited the reservation.

As the conversation about the piece of paper Ashley had found moved forward, Jim Red Feather divulged far more information than he had earlier. And it became crystal clear why the conversation had to take place at Wounded Knee.

"When we were at Wounded Knee in 1973, I saw a piece of torn paper from this same treaty," he said. "One of the men had been shot, and he was dying."

Jim told how the man, Dino, instructed his wife to pull a tightly wrapped packet from his boot. Protected in the packet was a piece of paper, smallish, about a four-inch square.

"As I knelt above him," he said softly, "I looked into his eyes. 'What is this, Dino?' I asked him.

"'It is part of a treaty,' the dying man said to me, gasping for air between words. 'Something my great-uncle gave me before he died,' he said, struggling. 'We don't know where the rest of it is. Another Sioux has part. I think here in Pine Ridge. We don't know . . .'

"Dino died without giving me any more information about the treaty. I looked at the paper briefly, but in the melee around us, I sealed it again and put it in my pocket.

"At the time, we were all uncertain of our future. I passed the piece of paper on to my son Ted because I did not know what to do with it then. That was years ago. Ted is over in Ogalstet working his farm—it is the peak of the season. What he has done with the paper, or if he still even has it, I cannot say."

The day was fading fast, and it was almost 5:00 P.M.

Leonard Jumping Bear stood and clasped his brother-in-law's shoulder. "You and the girls should go to Ogalstet," Leonard said to Jim. "I wish I could be more help, but this is the first I've heard of this. If the meaning of this is to unfold, it must be done as soon as possible. I know that years and years have passed. But would it not be awful to have the answers never be found because of a lapse now?"

Jim agreed but didn't want to take Robin and Denise because they had jobs to go to in Rapid City in the morning. Leonard offered to drive the girls home to Jim's daughter Gail's house. She'd had to work and couldn't make it to the gathering that day. Jim looked down at his boots, lost in a moment of thought.

"Come with me to Ted's," he said at last, addressing the Arlingtons.

Ashley and Adam exchanged a look. They didn't know what to say.

"Mr. Red Feather, I don't know if it's our place to intrude on this . . ." Mr. Arlington began to protest.

Jim slowly raised his hand to stop his objections. "You and your family have done right by us. Please come with me to my son's. I do not ask this of you lightly."

Another Piece

Jim gave directions to Mrs. Arlington and Adam, who would ride behind in the SUV. Ashley and her father would ride with Jim in his pickup. They would head on U.S. 18 to Pine Ridge and then continue slightly northwest to Ogala.

"The heater is not working," Jim said as Ashley climbed into the cramped space beside her father. She'd worn a sweatshirt tied around the waist of her jeans, and she untied it now and put it on against the growing chill of evening.

Jim Red Feather told Ashley and her father about his wife's death several years earlier. He also told them more about Wounded Knee's unparalleled history during the drive, which was less than an hour. Hearing the incredible stories, Ashley suddenly felt her day-to-day struggles and concerns back in D.C. shrink to nothing.

Arriving on a rough dirt road at Ted Red Feather's farm, the caravan of two vehicles found Ted at the entrance to his property, repairing some barbed wire that had come down over time.

Greetings and introductions were exchanged, and Jim asked his son about the piece of paper he had given Ted years earlier.

Ted was big, even bigger than Alex Arlington, at about six-foot-one and maybe two hundred pounds. He had the same sort of thick, black hair as his father, only there was no gray, and it was not long enough to pull back into a ponytail as it hung down barely past his neck beneath a teal and white bandana.

"Is it up in the house?" Jim asked Ted.

"No," Ted answered. Ashley felt uneasy. What if the paper was gone? All they had were stories passed down orally through the years. What if there was nothing left but the stories? Ted spoke again. "I found a very safe place for it."

"That is good," Jim said, nodding. A moment passed. "Where is it then?" he asked his son, exasperated.

"Mother Earth is watching it for us," Ted said with a wink. "But we're a ways from it. You want to go there now?"

"Now would be the very best time, son," Jim said.

Ted grabbed a couple of flashlights and two small shovels from his toolshed and hopped in the back of his father's truck. The Arlingtons prepared to follow in the SUV. The light was low, and soon it would be dark.

Ted banged on the window to the cab.

"Better put it in four-wheel drive, Dad," Ted said. As his father stopped to engage the four-wheel drive, Ted motioned to the Arlingtons' tires and held up four fingers to Mrs. Arlington, who quickly realized what Ted was getting at and pressed the dashboard button to put the SUV into four-wheel drive.

They proceeded over bumpy land, around plowed cropland on dirt roads with a tire track on each side and practically unmolested prairie in the middle of the road. They reached the end of what looked to be a cornfield where cattle were grazing.

"Right here!" Ted said as he rapped his knuckles against the glass in the back window of the cab.

Ted pulled a screwdriver and the two small shovels from the back of the truck as the Arlingtons grabbed two flashlights from the glovebox and climbed out of their vehicle. Jim carried his flashlights and walked side-by-side with Ted, with the Arlingtons walking respectfully behind.

"So, tell me what's going on," Ted said.

Jim told his part of the story, ending it with the unlikely way he hooked up with the Arlingtons at the convenience store. Ashley divulged what she knew as they walked through a ravine. With the flashlights all pointed forward, the rough ground was well lit. Jim picked up the rest of the story from the late afternoon meal at Wounded Knee.

"I've always wondered about that paper, Dad," Ted said. "Especially when I work out on this area of my property. You told me it was the start of some treaty, but not much else."

"I didn't have a lot of information myself, son," Jim said. "Except what I got from Dino."

"How are Dino's wife and kids?" Ted asked. "It's almost twenty-five years ago he died."

Jim nodded. "You were just a young man then. His family is well. Both of his children are working, one with the American Indian Movement and the other with the Bureau of Indian Affairs."

"I have no idea what AIM is up to these days," Ted said, referring to the activist group that had brought so much attention to the American Indian cause. "You can love them or hate them, depends what's going on. But that's good that one is with the BIA. They need more Indians in the BIA."

Ted stepped out of the ravine and stopped at the top, waving his flashlight at a series of green posts marking the end of his property and another series of gray posts only a few feet from the green ones, marking the beginning of his neighbor's property. He looked at one of the posts and even felt it with his hand.

"Hmm," Ted said. "Not this one." He went to the left and shined his light on the side of the third post. "Okay, this is it," Ted said. "If it's still here, it's down about two feet or so."

Adam offered to help. Ted had Ashley shine a light on the ground just at the base of the post Ted had identified by a dot of yellow paint no bigger than a quarter on the side near the top.

"Sprayed that yellow so I could find it again," Ted said with a smile. "Of course, it had been so long that I really forgot about it unless I was out here."

Adam dug into the ground, next to where Ted was digging.

"What are we looking for?" Adam asked.

"A piece of quartz that looks like a moccasin," Ted replied.

"None of this ground looks like it has ever been dug out before," Adam said.

"Adam, it's probably been years since anyone dug here," his mother said. "That's more than enough time for grass to grow."

"That's right," Ted said. "It's been two decades, not just years. Boy, we are lucky. We had some bad flooding last year. But this area is just high enough that it wasn't touched. We moved the horses out here with the cattle for about a week. Luckily, the ravine here took most of the water or this area would have been washed away. If I'd put it on the south end of the property we'd be looking for it in Nebraska right now."

Ted and his father shared a chuckle.

"Here it is!" Adam said. "The rock."

Adam tapped again with his shovel and carefully shoveled out the rest of the dirt, pulling a fine piece of gray quartz covered with moist soil out of the ground. It was about ten inches long and perhaps three inches wide.

"Good job," Ted said. "Here, we need to go deeper. I'll take over."

Jim looked at Ted. Adam backed up, staring at the ground, wondering what lay only another six inches or so deeper.

"The boy was doing fine," Jim said to Ted.

"You're right, Dad," Ted agreed. "And after I find a link of the chain, Adam can finish the job for us."

Adam brushed some of the dirt from his hands and knees. His mother put her arm on his shoulder. Ashley looked up at the sky, which was beginning to show the first of the evening stars.

"Look up there," Ashley said to her father. "There's a line of stars almost exactly above us."

"Some say those are the great leaders of our people," Jim Red Feather said. "They seem to be watching over us."

Ashley smiled, liking the notion.

Ted's shovel made a scraping sound. "Okay, good, there's the chain," he said, cleaning off a half dozen links of chain before standing up. "Here's the deal. The chain is connected to the post and then to a black metal box. That way, even with a flood, we would've had a shot to find it. Or if the post had been dug out or moved for some reason, we'd have probably found it. Inside the metal box is a plastic bag with a plastic container, which has everything inside it—another plastic bag, some white plastic wrapping, and the cardboard with the paper in it."

"So I can dig hard until I find it?" Adam asked, crouching down with the flashlights pointing toward where he was digging.

"Shouldn't be a problem," Ted said, brushing dirt off the knees of his jeans as he stood. He wiped some sweat from his forehead.

Adam dug for just a minute or two before hitting the small black box. Ted leaned down and pulled the chain up.

Ashley could hardly believe it. In a little black box miles from any town on the South Dakota prairie, this chase was taking another big step.

Ted worked the box until it opened. Inside was a clear plastic container, just as he had said. For all the excitement Ashley felt as she looked at Jim Red Feather, she knew she couldn't fully imagine how much another piece of the treaty must mean to him.

"Let's take this back to the house and open it there," Jim said. "I want to have a good long look at it."

Adam walked with his father, and Ashley walked next to her mother, bringing up the rear. Ted led the way as Jim followed behind him, holding the plastic container in his hands, close to his heart.

"Do you know that this is not just for Jim but for his people too?" Mrs. Arlington spoke softly to Ashley.

Ashley nodded. "I know, Mom," she whispered. "I know there's no way for me to feel what it's like to be an American Indian. But after hearing Mr. Red Feather talk about the massacre at Wounded Knee, it seems like it was more than just that people died that day. It's like their dream died too. The whole Ghost Dance thing, where friends would be together again and the earth would be left alone and beautiful . . ." she looked at her mother. "Do you know what I mean?"

"I know, honey," her mother whispered.

The Safe-Deposit Box

"It's not much, but it's our home," Ted said as they passed in front of him into the tiny house. Ted's wife, Stephanie, did not appear to be Indian, but Ted volunteered that she was one-eighth Lakota.

Jim sat at the kitchen table, where he opened the clear container and took out the plastic bag. He got all the way down to the cardboard that held what was supposed to be the document. He bowed his head and grabbed his son's hand, who in turned grabbed Stephanie's hand. In Lakota, Jim prayed for a minute. The Arlingtons bowed their heads while Jim Red Feather spoke quietly.

When he was done, he looked up and pulled the worn cardboard back. He unfolded the document and placed it next to the copy of the one the Arlingtons had given him. Just then, Mr. Arlington pulled out a packet he'd brought from the car.

"Here," he said, unpacking the original square of the treaty and putting it out on the table next to the second piece. "I think we need the real thing for this."

Jim nodded and fit the papers together. This section was not, as the Arlingtons—especially Ashley—had hoped, the right-hand side that would continue the sentences on the piece Ashley found. Rather, this was the bottom left-hand portion. It was obvious that the paper had been torn in half at least twice—and hopefully not any more times.

At what appeared to be the bottom of the page was lettering identifying it as an official government document, binding for the people and government of the United States.

"Look there, where the two pieces of paper meet," Adam said.

Sure enough, one of the signatures that had not been completely visible on the first piece of the treaty was now made clear. The Sioux name spilled over from the bottom of the paper the Arlingtons had found to the top of Jim's paper. Red Jumping Bear was the name, Jim said. The "Bear" part alone meant nothing conclusively to Jim because a lot of Sioux had "Bear" in their name. And the Jumping Bear family alone had hundreds of family members, not including the hundreds, maybe thousands of others at one time who had "Bear" in their name.

"Red Jumping Bear was Leonard's great-uncle," Jim said, his natural reserve falling away in his excitement. "I know that name. He was friends with our family."

"Was he a leader, Father?" Ted asked.

"He was a chief, but only for a short period of time," Jim said.

"Why only a short time?" Ashley asked.

"He was killed in 1890 at the Wounded Knee Massacre," Jim replied.

The Arlingtons were quiet. The story was intertwined with Wounded Knee and had more turns than the caves at Wind Cave National Park.

Later, Jim Red Feather called Leonard Jumping Bear and told him of his great-uncle's signature on the treaty.

"Leonard, do you know of any of his family anywhere?" Jim asked into the phone.

Jim nodded and grunted in response to whatever Leonard was saying on the other end of the phone. Finally he pulled a pen out of his front pocket and jotted a number down.

"The bank in Hot Springs? Yes, I know where it is. . . . Yes, Leonard, we will let you know. Good night now."

"We have little to go on," Jim said to the group in the kitchen. "Jumping Bear lost just about everyone over the years, including plenty at Wounded Knee.

"Leonard's family, they sort of lost contact with the reservation, since there were only a couple of them left, and their ties to the Sioux started to slip more and more with each generation." Jim shook his head.

"There is one known Jumping Bear descendant left besides Leonard," he said. "He is the vice president of a bank in Hot Springs. His name is Robert Jones, but his birth name was Robert Jumping Bear. His father died young, and Robert was adopted by a white ranching family when he was a little boy. Leonard said he met him once on the reservation a few years back. Said he is a good man, just not much into the Sioux way."

"Let's go!" Adam said.

"Come on, Adam," his father chided. "This isn't our decision to make."

"So, what should we do?" Mrs. Arlington asked. "Do you want to go to Hot Springs, or call this Robert Jones tomorrow? Let us know how we can help."

Jim looked at Ted. But knowing he had far more work on the farm than he could handle already, Ted shook his head.

"At this time of the year and with everything going on here at Pine Ridge, I don't know if I'll have time. We don't have a lot of help here, is all," Ted explained, an arm around his wife.

Jim nodded. "Alex, Anne—you and the children have done right by us, as I have said. We trust you, and since you have offered to help, we would like to accept if you are certain you want to pursue this with us."

"Of course we'll help," Mr. Arlington assured them. "We feel honored to have your trust."

Jim arranged to meet the Arlingtons at a certain diner in Hot Springs the next morning. Mrs. Arlington would call the bank in the morning to set up an appointment, and they planned to meet for breakfast and take it from there.

"What about the originals?" Mrs. Arlington asked. "Do you want to keep them?"

Jim looked at the two pieces of paper on the table. They were wrinkled, a bit dirty, and brittle to the point that they could break apart at any second. This piece of history was as frail as any antique vase. And if this paper was torn any more, it would be very difficult to make sense of it. "It might be helpful if you would keep the originals with you for now—I know you will return them to us when this is all over," he suggested.

The pieces of the treaty were sealed carefully in a plastic page protector and locked in Mr. Arlington's briefcase. Jim wrote down Ted and Stephanie's phone number along with his own. The families embraced, and after Jim had a longer good-bye with his son and daughter-in-law, he pulled out behind the Arlingtons. They could see the headlights of his truck in the distance behind them as they headed back to their motor home at Wind Cave.

The following morning, Anne Arlington led the family in a run around the camping area at Wind Cave. They did several laps. On other vacations they would have run farther, but with so many buffalo lining the road just outside the camping area, that wasn't a good idea.

After showering, Mrs. Arlington called the bank in Hot Springs and was able to set up an afternoon appointment with Robert Jones. Then she called Jim to give him an update. There was no answer.

"He must've already left to meet us in Hot Springs," she said. "And that means we'd better get a move on," she added, playfully swatting Adam with a towel.

An hour later, they were sitting at the diner, waiting for Jim Red Feather to show up. Mr. Arlington called Jim's house—again, no answer. Then he dialed Ted's number. Stephanie answered the phone.

"Oh, Alex, I'm so glad you called," she began. "I'm afraid we have some bad news over here. This morning Jim got up early, like he always does, and felt some pain—he's had a heart attack," Stephanie explained. "He called us, and we called an ambulance. Ted's with him at the hospital in Rapid City now."

Mr. Arlington got all the details Stephanie could give him and then promised to call later in the day. He went back to the booth where his family was waiting and filled them in on Jim Red Feather's condition. They reacted with a mix of shock and sadness.

None of the four felt very hungry, but they ordered breakfast anyway. As they finished eating, Mrs. Arlington asked, "What can we do for Jim?"

"There's not much anyone can do in this situation," said Mr. Arlington.

"Wait," Ashley interrupted. "Didn't I see a floral shop a few doors down? We could send Mr. Red Feather a small bouquet or something just to let him know we're thinking about him."

"Great idea, Ash!" exclaimed Adam, already heading for the door.

After Mr. Arlington paid the bill at the diner, the four walked over to the floral shop. They had a mixed arrangement of colorful flowers sent to the hospital with a note expressing their concern.

Rather than mope about town, Mr. Arlington decided to try to improve the mood by suggesting the family go experience the hot springs the town was noted for.

"The Sioux and Cheyenne tribes used to go to the natural hot springs to soak away their worries and pains," he said. "Let's go take our minds off everything else."

The idea turned out to be a good one. The drive through the rolling hills was beautiful, and the eighty-seven-degree water ran both inside and outside of the hills. Adam entertained the family with his wild trips down the water slides at Evans Plunge. Coincidentally, the Arlingtons learned the Plunge was built by Fred Evans in 1890, the same year as the Wounded Knee Massacre.

The family dried off and went to the Mammoth Site Museum, built over a dry ancient sinkhole. Adam and Ashley were astounded by the fossils of more than fifty woolly mammoths that had died there thousands of years before.

"How awful—the sinkhole was filled with spring water, and when animals came to drink, they were sucked in and trapped!" Ashley exclaimed.

"I know," Adam agreed. "It's kind of gory. But they had to die some time. And now we get to see them here, all in one place. This one's amazing!" he said, pointing to the skeleton of a mammoth whose shoulder height was over thirteen feet.

"It says here there are twenty-seven other species of animals from the Ice Age accounted for here," Mr. Arlington said in wonder. "Amazing. And the silt in the sinkhole preserved the fossils."

After their tour there was over, the Arlingtons decided to head to the quaint downtown area in Hot Springs for a late lunch, since their stomachs were telling them it was time to eat. Adam brought in his computer, and after ordering four burgers, the family watched Adam work.

"See, I downloaded copies of all these files," Adam said. "Let me run a search on Jumping Bear."

The computer's cursor turned into an hourglass, and it ransacked the documents in search of Jumping Bear. It showed two references on the screen.

"Jackpot!" Adam said. He scrolled through both references. Red Jumping Bear was indeed a highly regarded chief but only for a short period of time because of his untimely death. The chief had associations with both Sitting Bull and Crazy Horse at one time or another. Adam scrolled through the documents but couldn't find anything else. After a big lunch, the Arlingtons headed over to the Hot Springs National Bank, just a couple blocks away, stopping first at the post office where they made copies of the two pieces of the treaty lined up perfectly on the copier.

Robert Jones welcomed the Arlingtons into his office promptly at 2:00 P.M. After making the introductions, Ashley began to explain the chain of events that had led them there, including the recent heart attack that prevented Jim from accompanying them. When she mentioned the pieces of the torn treaty, Jones, a tall, dark-skinned man with brown hair, wearing a sharp olive green suit and suspenders, sat bolt upright in his chair, a look of complete surprise brightening his face.

"You have got to be kidding me!" Jones said, putting his hands on his desk and pushing himself up as though he had been shot out of his seat by a cannon. "Come with me!"

They followed Jones out of his office. He walked quickly across the lobby of the bank and behind the teller stations. After asking a teller to help him and the Arlingtons into the safe-deposit box vault, Jones fished in his pocket for his keys, but after looking through about ten keys on the ring, put them back in his pocket.

"Stay here for just a second," Jones said. "I left the one to the safe-deposit box in the lockbox in my office."

Jones was practically running by now.

"What do you think he knows about this?" Adam asked.

In a moment, Robert Jones was back, fairly panting from rushing. He began to search the numbers on the boxes at a furious pace.

"This bank was built in 1910," Jones said, speaking quietly, almost as if muttering to himself. "The first safe-deposit box ever taken out here was taken by my grandpa. My father died when I was a little boy, and he left it to me.

"But my father said Grandpa told him never to open it until he was told to. The will stipulated the same instructions for me. And for me to give my children the same instructions. I thought that was so odd. But anyway, when

I was adopted by another family, they honored the will and left the box untouched. When I came to work here at the bank, though, I couldn't resist the temptation to find out what was inside. I couldn't figure out who would ever tell me to open it anyway," he shrugged. "I didn't understand what was so special about what I found, but now that I've heard your story I think there's more significance to this than I'd imagined."

As Jones spoke about his blood ancestors and his adopted family, Ashley wondered what the man thought of his Sioux heritage.

"Are you still . . . I mean, do you consider yourself to be a Sioux?" Ashley asked Jones.

Jones stopped for a second, turned around, and smiled.

"You know, my wife and I visited the reservation some time ago," Jones said. "That's probably how you ended up finding me. I met Leonard Jumping Bear, a member of my family."

"We met Leonard," Adam said.

"It breaks my heart what's going on now on the reservation. In some ways, it is starting to get better. But for a time, I was afraid to go out there. I just saw so many problems—alcoholism, poverty—so many that I didn't think I could make a difference no matter how hard I worked."

"How about just making a small difference then?" Ashley asked.

"Ashley, I don't believe that is your concern," her mother said sharply.

"No, Ashley's right," Jones said. "Not even a week ago, I brought it to our board of directors here at the bank.

We're going to start doing more business with the Sioux on the reservation. They have a few projects that they really need some money up front for, and the ideas I've heard about sound good. If this works as a sort of pilot program, we could extend it to the other reservations in the state. It's strange, because I've always had a social conscience for all minorities—except for my own. But I want my children to learn about their heritage, and they will. It's just like where you kids came from; have you been back to the country of your ancestors?"

Adam and Ashley shook their heads.

"Well, see?" Jones said. "At the same time, I have less of an excuse because I'm so close to where I came from, with Pine Ridge just down the hill. My wife has a little Cheyenne in her, and we've both made a pledge to learn more about our heritages. It's what makes us who we are."

Jones kept searching for the number of the box and found it. He put the key in and turned the lock. Jones pulled the box out and set it on the table. He opened the box to reveal a small folded piece of paper.

"Another part of the treaty!" Ashley exclaimed. "That's what this is!"

"Go ahead, take it out," Jones told Ashley.

She unfolded it and pulled from her pocket the copy she had made of the other two pieces. The piece was about four inches wide by just more than six inches high. It lined up perfectly beside the Arlingtons' piece and part of Jim's piece.

"Looks like there's still one piece left," Ashley said.

They looked at Jones's piece alone at first.

The bottom of the piece had complete sentences in it as the type broke off to the right in a single narrow column

On this 1st day of January, 18__, the government of the United States of America and all American Indians agree to the terms and conditions of this treaty, which is binding here in this form, and will be formalized within the following two days. This treaty finalizes all arrangements to the ultimate resolution of gold and land rights to the Black Hills in the United States of America. As of this day, until a time 11 years from now on the first day of January, 1885, when the Sioux Nation is to assume full control of the Black Hills. The U.S. government assumes all land rights to the Black Hills. As of January 1, 1885, no white man shall be allowed in the Black Hills. All rail lines must be withdrawn by the U.S. government, and all roads will be left to the Indians to do what they wish as they see fit.

Until the 1st day of January, 1885, no white man is to be harassed or troubled by Indians. All mining activity can continue endlessly until 11 years from this day of January, 1875, until the

General George Crook

Captain William Grattan

Chon-gah-ma-ho-to-haas-ka

Wah-ko-ke-yan-gah-tah

Ma-to-ka-in-yan-ke

Official Document of the government of the United States of America. Contents are said to be binding for the United States of America, all of its people, and the U.S. government across the page from the signatures of the U.S. representatives and the American Indian representatives.

Ashley carefully laid the new piece onto the copy of the other two pieces. No one uttered a sound as Robert Jones read the document aloud:

"On this 1st day of January, 1875, the government of the United States of America and all American Indians agree to the terms and conditions of this treaty, which is binding here in this form, and will be formalized within the following two days. This treaty finalizes all arrangements as to the ultimate resolution of gold and land rights to the Black Hills in the United States of America. As of this day, until a time 10 years from now on the first day of January, 1885, when the Sioux Nation is to assume full control of the Black Hills. The U.S. government assumes all land rights to the Black Hills. As of January 1, 1885, no white man shall be allowed in the Black Hills. All rail lines must be withdrawn by the U.S. government, and all roads will be left to the Indians to do what they wish as they see fit."

The Arlingtons and Robert Jones looked at each other, and then he continued to read the one narrow paragraph of text, which ended abruptly at a tear in the paper.

"Until the 1st day of January, 1885, no white man is to be harassed or troubled by Indians. All mining activity can continue endlessly until 10 years from this day of January, 1875, until the . . ." Jones looked up. "That's it."

"Wow!" Adam proclaimed. "That means the Indians would still own the Black Hills today!"

"Still, it's not much of a deal," Ashley said. "In ten years of mining, the land would have been eaten up. But who knows?"

Mr. Arlington noted the date that the Black Hills would have reverted to Indian ownership—1885.

"So this would have given the land back just five years before the Wounded Knee Massacre. Makes you kind of wonder if the Wounded Knee Massacre in 1890—or the incident in 1973, for that matter—if they'd have happened if this had become the law."

"Just think if the Indians still had the Black Hills," Robert Jones said. "This bank wouldn't be here," Jones said. "I wonder where the rest of the treaty is."

It was still impossible to figure out all of the signatures, although the one was definitely Captain Gratton, and the first two of the Indians' names concluded on the piece of paper Jones had provided.

"Do you know who that is?" Ashley asked Jones.

"I wish I did," Jones said. "I have to admit I really don't know as much about the Sioux language and culture as I should."

The five headed back to Jones's office. As he passed the receptionist, she held out a handful of pink message slips.

Jones looked back at the Arlingtons. "Amazing what a little piece of paper will do for you, isn't it?" he said with a smile.

They went into Jones's office, stopping at the copy machine to make several clean copies of the three pieces of the treaty reunited on the page. Jones closed the door, and they sat down.

"This is starting to look like a real treaty," Adam exclaimed.

"It sure is," his mother said. "You know, now is the time to start thinking about our next step. Any ideas?"

"How about I call a lawyer I know with the Bureau of Indian Affairs to see what we can find out?" Alex asked. "You should know up front, though, the BIA is a government agency."

"And I'm not even sure they'd be interested," Mrs. Arlington said. "I mean, this treaty seems important to us as a quest and as a piece of history. But it's not as if it will turn back time or become the law now."

Everyone looked at Robert Jones. "Mr. Jones, what are your thoughts?"

"Well—you folks have been doing pretty well so far, I'd say. Jim Red Feather and Leonard Jumping Bear have done well to have you on the trail."

Adam and Ashley looked at each other and shared a smile. They'd been afraid the search might have to end here.

"How about we head back to the Crazy Horse Monument and see if anyone there can give us some more information," Ashley proposed.

"Like what?" Jones asked.

"Maybe like who the Sioux woman was who dropped off the books," Ashley answered. "Maybe she could give us a name or something, or at least someone to talk to."

"Sounds good," Mrs. Arlington agreed. "Plus, we could find out the names of the other two Indians who signed the treaty since none of us reads Lakota."

"And then maybe one of their ancestors knows something about this, right?" Adam asked excitedly.

"Let's hope so," Mrs. Arlington said.

Chapter 6

The General's Letter

Robert Jones entrusted the third piece of the treaty to the Arlingtons for the time being and wished them well, and after agreeing to be in touch, the family headed back toward Crazy Horse.

Everyone in the SUV was developing scenarios of what might have happened had the Indians regained and kept control of the Black Hills.

"All right," Mr. Arlington began. "Let's say the treaty was honored, and the Black Hills, likely stripped of all the gold and other precious minerals, reverted to the Indians. What next?"

Adam spoke up first. "I don't think the Wounded Knee Massacre would have taken place. The Sioux would have had their sacred land back, and the area would have been big enough to keep a good supply of buffalo."

Ashley shook her head. "I think the Wounded Knee Massacre *would* have still happened, or something else like it, at some point," she said, looking out the window. "But having the Indians back in control of the Black Hills would have slowed the settlers on the way to the northwest."

"It's hard to imagine the Black Hills as a reservation," her mother interjected. "I don't think the whites or the government would have had the patience to constantly bypass the Black Hills when traveling or setting up towns just outside the hills. There would have been raids by white settlers or miners still looking for gold, timber, or something like that. How would those intrusions be handled? It could have sparked a war, meant the destruction of the Black Hills, or something similar."

"Hey—no Black Hills means no Mount Rushmore," Adam pointed out.

"Hmm," Ashley said. "That's quite a thought. And the Crazy Horse Monument was inspired by Mount Rushmore, at least from the actual sculpting point of view."

"So no Crazy Horse Monument," Adam said. "But, wait!" he continued, punching the keys on his keyboard. "It says here that Crazy Horse died in 1877. So, if the treaty had been enacted, maybe he would have never left the area to surrender at Fort Robinson and join a reservation. Maybe he would have lived!"

"That's possible," his father agreed. "The lives of a lot of famous leaders, both white and American Indian, would have changed."

"What about Custer?" Adam asked, looking up from his computer screen. "What would have happened to him? He wasn't killed at the Little Bighorn by Crazy Horse and the others until June of 1876."

"Right," his mother mused. "From what I've read, Custer was on a fast track up until he died. He was supposedly getting in a position where he could someday be president."

"Can you imagine that?" Ashley said, her blue eyes sparkling. "If this treaty had been kept for even a couple of decades, and then they still pushed forward with the monuments in the Black Hills, Custer's face could have ended up on Mount Rushmore!"

As the foursome arrived at Crazy Horse Monument, a thought crossed Mrs. Arlington's mind when she spotted the telephone near the entrance.

"Think we should call Ted or Jim, or should we wait?" she asked the family.

"I think we should call and find out how Mr. Red Feather's doing," Ashley said.

Mr. Arlington called the hospital in Rapid City but was told Jim was in the intensive care unit and that the hospital could not give out any additional information. He asked that Ted Red Feather be paged. Several minutes passed before he came on the line.

"Hello; this is Ted Red Feather."

"Ted, this is Alex Arlington. My family and I were wondering how your father is doing."

"Good to hear from you, Alex. He's not completely out of the woods yet, but he's in stable condition, and the doctors believe he'll make a full recovery," Ted said. "Any news from the search?"

"Actually, yes, there is news—we've got a third piece of the treaty."

"Fantastic! So you found Robert Jumping Bear?" Ted asked.

"Right; we talked to Robert Jones at the bank," Mr. Arlington said. "Turns out he'd been given a big part of the treaty—a key piece, it looks like—but never realized what he had." He explained how Robert Jones had been given the key to the safe-deposit box at his own bank, a box that was opened in 1910 to put the paper in and then opened only once before today.

"That's incredible," Ted said.

"It gets better," Mr. Arlington said. "Ted, the treaty says that the U.S. government was going to have complete control of the Black Hills with no Indian interference from 1875 until 1885. But on January 1, 1885, the Black Hills were supposed to be returned to the Indians with the government tearing out the railroad lines and everything. The whole thing, everything left in the Black Hills, was supposed to go back to the Lakota people."

"Well, my father will be very interested to hear this—I'll share your discovery with him when he's able to talk."

Mr. Arlington hung up the phone and turned at the sound of loud footsteps getting closer.

"Dad! Dad!" Ashley cried, as she ran toward her father. "Hurry, we have to go. They're looking for us!"

Ashley was out of breath after sprinting across the parking lot from the gift shop where she and her mother had gone to browse during her father's phone call. Before he could get a word out, Ashley continued.

"Dad, you and Adam have to come in the gift shop with Mom and me," she said, still breathing hard. "General Crook's great-great-grandson—the one who spoke at Mount Rushmore—came here looking for us!"

Adam and his father walked quickly back into the gift shop, catching up with Mrs. Arlington, who was talking to the older Indian woman behind the counter.

"Go ahead, Rose, fill them in too, if you don't mind," Anne Arlington said.

"Well, the other day you asked me about whether there were any books with treaty information in them, and I told you about Mr. Crook speaking at Mount Rushmore . . . do you remember that?" Rose asked.

The Arlingtons all nodded yes.

"Not five minutes before closing that night, a man and his wife came in," Rose said. "He asked if I knew of anyone looking for information about a treaty that his ancestor, General Crook, wrote about. Well, of course, at the time it didn't ring a bell. Then this man told me that the folks who asked about it while he was speaking that day at Mount Rushmore had on Crazy Horse T-shirts, blue ones. That prodded my memory, and I remembered you buying two of those shirts for your children."

"I can't believe we missed him," Ashley said disappointedly. "Do you think he had information for us?"

"Well, I don't know about that," Rose said. "But he did leave a card with his number and address over in Aberdeen."

"Aberdeen?" Adam said. "That's clear on the other side of the state, isn't it?"

"Yes, it is," Rose said. "But here's his number if you want it."

"Thank you for your time, ma'am," Ashley said as she took the card and headed out the door with her family.

They headed back to the motor home, tired from the trip but with too much adrenaline to slow down.

"Can we call him now?" Ashley prodded.

Her mother smiled and agreed to make the call on her cell phone. Elijah Crook was at home, and after she explained that she and her family were the ones asking about the treaty that was never enacted, he was eager to talk. He told her that he'd had General Crook's letter sent out to him from Washington.

They arranged to meet the next afternoon at Elijah Crook's home in Aberdeen to share what information they had.

Adam pulled out his computer, popped up the screen, and figured the best route possible to take to Aberdeen the next day. Then, exhausted after an eventful day, everyone was ready for bed.

After a quick breakfast, the family headed out early the next morning in a rambling southwest to northeast line. About halfway to Aberdeen they crossed gigantic Lake Oahe, at Oahe Dam, part of the Missouri River system. Ashley flipped through their South Dakota guide and learned that the Oahe Dam and Lake had been dedicated by President John F. Kennedy in 1962.

"The name Oahe comes from the Lakota word that roughly translated means 'a foundation' or 'a place to stand on,'" Ashley pointed out. "And check this out," she went on. "Lewis and Clark's Shoshone Indian guide, Sacajawea, is supposedly buried near Lake Oahe, at the Fort Manual Trading Post."

Adam spotted some fishing boats on the water. "Hey, Dad, we should come back here and show Mom and Ashley who's better at fishing," he said, referring to an ongoing family competition.

Ashley and her mother laughed. "You're on, pal," Ashley said.

"Ah, they rise to the bait, as it were," Mr. Arlington joked.

The family was a bit road-weary as they pulled into Aberdeen. They found the county road Mr. Crook had told them to take, and not four miles down the road—the final mile of which was a dirt road—found his spacious ranch home. Mrs. Arlington drove slowly over the cattle guard between the posts at the entrance to the driveway of the home.

Elijah Crook met came riding up on a tall, chestnut-colored horse to greet them.

"Thanks for coming all the way out here," he said. "Just pull on up there. I'll go put Charger back in the barn and be right up to join you at the house."

The Arlingtons waited on the porch of the house until Mr. Crook arrived, snapping a pair of riding gloves against his thigh. "Come on in," he motioned, holding the door to the house for the Arlingtons.

The Arlingtons were intrigued by the house's decor as soon as they walked in the door. Mr. Crook remarked that his two children were in school that day and that his wife, a teacher at the high school in Aberdeen, was also gone. He led them down a hallway where four steps led down to a big living room decorated in a western motif.

"Come on into the study," he said, guiding them through a door off the living room. "Let me show you the general."

"The general" turned out to be a two-foot-high portrait of General George Crook. Elijah Crook explained that the general was called the "Gray Fox" by the Indians. His graying hair, intelligent eyes, and sharp military uniform gave the portrait an air of dignity.

"It's the original," Elijah Crook said proudly, gazing at the glass-encased portrait. "It's all my family has from him. Everything else is either in Washington or in a museum. Actually, at one time, we had a pistol of his, but it's in a museum now. All we really wanted was the picture."

"I remember you mentioning it during the talk at Mount Rushmore, Mr. Crook," Mrs. Arlington said.

"Oh, please—it's Elijah," he insisted.

The portrait was in a gold frame with George Crook's name and rank engraved at the bottom along with the fact that he had died in 1890—the same year as the Wounded Knee Massacre.

"We did the frame," Elijah said. "We wanted to make sure this thing lasted forever."

"It's very impressive," Mr. Arlington said. "He looks like a true leader."

"Yes, and those were some rough times," Elijah said. "When he wasn't battling the Indians, he was battling the weather. It was always something. Supplies seemed to always be scarce, and the morale of the men swung like a pendulum. He had a tough job because he really did understand and respect the Indians. But his sworn duty was to his country, and he was a good soldier. He was a conflicted man."

Adam could not get over the eyes in the portrait. "It is almost like he's staring at us," he whispered.

"Don't worry, Adam," joked Ashley. "I'll protect you."

Elijah led them out into the comfortable living room and invited them to make themselves at home. While the Arlingtons studied the numerous books and artifacts around the room, he retreated to the kitchen to prepare sandwiches and soda for his guests. Upon reentering the room and offering the refreshments to the family, he walked over to the brick fireplace and lifted a box from the deep cedar mantle above it.

"This is the letter," he said, pulling out a wooden clipboardlike object with the letter on top, encased in a sort of fiberglass case. "And here's a photocopy for you to look at."

He gave one to each of the Arlingtons. "The photocopy is a little easier to read," he said. "I've filled in some of the missing ink with a pen, which really makes it clearer."

The years had taken a toll on the letter, dated January 5, 1875, but it was still legible:

Dear General Sherman,

We have offered the Indians the deal that met your approval, as well as the government's. We procured a signed and sealed document, with three chiefs' signatures and both mine and Captain Gratton's. At last I felt as though we had done the right thing. These Black Hills are sacred to the Natives. I still question whether our actions have been justified. I am first a soldier, and I have never questioned my duty to the U.S. Government. But to my God, I have often wondered how we are serving Him with our policy in the West.

I write today to inform you that the treaty has failed. We had met with the Indians on the south end of the Black Hills. We sent word to gather as many chiefs as possible to consider our proposal for control of the Paha Sapa—the Black Hills.

Three chiefs joined us: Jumping Bear, High Wolf, and Fire Thunder. Crazy Horse declined the meeting. But the chiefs negotiated very little and seemed pleased with the plan for the government to have rights to the land for a period of ten years, after which time the land would be returned, without rancor, to the Indians.

The treaty was signed, and we planned to meet again in two days' time, time enough to arrange further details. All seemed well, and the chiefs offered to smoke with us. But then, shots were fired from a wooded area. We still do not know what caused the man or men to fire, nor at what they were firing. We are missing three soldiers at present— deserters, or dead. When the Indians heard the shots, they assumed the bullets were meant for them, as they have been so many times in the past. I beseeched the chiefs come with me to my quarters where they would be safe.

Jumping Bear appeared to embrace the idea, but at that moment, we lost control. Fire Thunder was shot dead, and High Wolf took hold of the treaty and tore it up, throwing the pieces to the wind. Jumping Bear clasped a piece of the torn paper, but the other pieces blew away from me as I was forced to evacuate to camp and safety. Fighting intensified the next day, and all three regiments broke camp and headed back to their respective posts. Instead of goodwill, it seems as though hostilities have only risen since our latest, and to this date, our best, offering. The treaty, but for a piece I managed to catch and a piece Jumping Bear may still have, has been lost on the prairie, blowing away with what might be our last glimmer of hope for peace with these people.

The tensions are now higher than ever, and all under my command await another battle any and every day the sun rises.

Sir, I wish I had better news to report. But five days into this new year, the hands of time are hostage to the anger between two cultures. I pray for a peaceful solution, but I will not risk my men's safety. It appears this latest turn of events has put us past the point of no return. With the words we are hearing from Crazy Horse through intermediaries, I feel certain that violence is on the horizon. I pray that this time, I am wrong.

I believe it is too late for treaties now. Let us hope future leaders will succeed where we have tried and failed. In hopes that the future will bring understanding, I can only say to those who will know me: Look deep into my eyes and judge kindly our vain efforts.

General George Crook

"Man, that's something," Adam said, looking up from the letter.

"The general shipped this painting home the day after he mailed this letter from what we can tell," Elijah Crook said. "The portrait was done in the field out west—that's why it's so small. In those days these kinds of formal portraits were much larger. Anyway, he had it mounted himself and sent it back east. Maybe he thought his days were numbered, or maybe he wanted to capture the spirit of the times 'in situ' as the painters say."

Ashley's mind was doing a hundred miles an hour. Although she was as interested in the topic as anyone in the family, she hadn't said a word.

"What is it, Ashley?" her father asked. "What are you thinking about?"

"I think I have the answer," Ashley said, standing up. "I know what General Crook is telling us!"

Behind the General's Eyes

Ashley asked everyone to follow her back into the room where the portrait was.

"Can you take it off the wall so we can see it from the back?" Ashley asked, breathless with excitement.

Mr. Crook seemed reluctant. "I don't see why not, I guess," he said, and after a moment's hesitation he took the picture down from the wall.

Ashley studied the painting. "The way it's mounted, you can only see the burlap from the side," she observed. "Any chance you could open the case?"

"I don't know about that," he said. "Keeping it airtight has helped protect the painting from the environment, fluctuations of temperature . . ."

"Ashley," her father said firmly. "Tell us what you're thinking. Mr. Crook isn't going to open this thing up on a whim, honey. If he has more to go on, he can decide if we really need to open the frame."

"Look at the letter," Ashley said impatiently. "He wrote, 'Look deep into my eyes.' He knew that General Sherman couldn't look into his eyes in this picture—because he sent the picture to his family. He sent that picture probably the day after he sent the letter to General Sherman. Why would he do that? What was the rush on the picture?"

"So you think there's an answer in the picture itself?" Mr. Crook asked Ashley.

"Yes, I do," Ashley answered. "There's got to be something he wanted his family to know—and to judge him kindly, like the letter said. I just know it's the final piece of the treaty—it was the best he could do to preserve some small sign that he'd tried to do what he thought was right."

"You know, I think she's on to something," Elijah said to the Arlingtons.

But Mr. Arlington still wasn't sure. "Why didn't he send a copy of the letter to his family then?" he asked. "I mean, if this whole thing is part of the treaty, and he wanted his family to make sense of it, why not include them from the very beginning? How would they ever make the connection to the letter?"

"That's a good question," Elijah replied, rubbing his chin. He leaned forward then, as though a thought had just come to him. "He couldn't have sent a letter like that to his family. That was official army correspondence, so it would have been classified at one level or another. It would have been a form of treason to let a civilian see something like that." A spark of excitement lit his face.

"You know," he went on, "if this is part of a puzzle, maybe the General didn't want it assembled until long after he was gone. In the letter, it seems like he'd come to realize no treaty would work—this was his last effort. Maybe the army changed its mind about the treaty. Maybe the government decided it had made a mistake in the first place or would make a mistake in reopening the issue down the road. Maybe he sensed the time wasn't right, and no one was supposed to see this for a hundred years."

"If that's the case," Mrs. Arlington said with a grin, "then the General sure got his wish."

They all smiled as Mr. Crook put the picture on the carpeted floor, face up. With Mr. Arlington holding it, Elijah pulled out the screws that kept it locked into the frame.

He pulled the painting out gently, never touching the portrait itself with his hands, putting his fingers instead only on the burlap back of the picture.

"Here, Ashley," Mr. Crook said, holding the picture up high with the face of the general toward the ceiling. "Get underneath here and look for a second."

Ashley bent her knees and turned her head to the side. She could see several layers of burlap covering the back of the painting, but not much else. Gently, she reached with her hands.

Ashley prodded the back of the picture with her fingers. The burlap gave in quite a bit until she neared the area behind where Elijah indicated General Crook's eyes were located. There, she felt a noticeably thicker area, almost as if a tea bag or something was inside.

"Right here!" Ashley said, trying to control her enthusiasm and not shake Mr. Crook's hands as he held the picture. "There's some sort of gathering of the material here."

"What should we do, Mr. Crook?" Adam asked.

"I'll get a hunting knife," he said. "Can you hold this, Anne?"

"Of course," she said, putting her hands on the back of the picture near where he had held his.

Elijah returned with a soft blanket and a small, sharp knife. Carefully, he laid the portrait on its face, protected by the blanket.

"This might not be the best way to go about this, so we must be extra careful," Elijah explained. "We'll just do the best we can, and I'll take responsibility—I know how awful you'd feel if one of you damaged the painting."

Elijah cut wider than he needed to, leaving plenty of room around what appeared to be a lump sealed behind the burlap. Very carefully, he cut through the layers of burlap. The material was old and dusty, and it gave off a thin mist of dust as the knife pierced it each time.

"I've got something here," he said, flipping back a piece of the burlap to reveal a small pouch.

Elijah held the pouch carefully between his thumb and index finger, and cut carefully around it to release it from the burlap. The pouch was about two inches square. He trimmed it clean from the rest of the burlap and set it down.

"Well, look at what we have here," Adam said. The pouch was stitched shut and sealed with what looked to be a sort of molasses.

"Amazing this thing didn't come open already," Mrs. Arlington said. "Or that insects didn't get to it."

"Actually, it's not a coincidence at all that it's in great shape," Elijah said. "This thing carried more papers with it along its journey than a new car. When I got it, it came with a list of who had it and when. For some reason, the right sort of people in my family had it over the past century and a quarter. It has always been displayed properly from what I can tell by the notes I have and by the condition of the picture itself."

"Let's get this thing open!" Adam exclaimed excitedly, tiring of looking at the small leather pouch.

Elijah Crook picked up the pouch in his left hand and the knife in his right and started carefully snipping the pouch open, stitch by tiny stitch. He looked up at the Arlingtons, who were staring intently at his hands, and smiled.

"You know something," he said. "I'd be delighted if you'd take a turn, Ashley."

Ashley smiled.

"That's nice of you, Mr. Crook," she said. "But this is from a relative of yours."

"Please," he said, handing the pouch to her and then picking up the knife and holding it out to her, handle first. "Besides, I'm getting tired!"

Ashley grinned and started working carefully on the pouch, just as Mr. Crook had done, stitch by stitch. There must have been thirty stitches holding the pouch closed. And in some places the sticky substance was holding the leather tightly closed while in others barely a trace of it was noticeable. Ashley worked for more than ten minutes on it as the group sat silently.

"Maybe," Elijah said with a sly grin, "it wasn't supposed to be opened for another hundred years."

"That's good," Ashley replied with a big smile, "because it might take me that long to get it open."

Ashley started again. She was getting closer to the end.

Ashley popped the final stitch. She turned her palm down and set the pouch on the glass table. She carefully lifted her left hand up to make sure nothing was sticking to it. One of the pieces of leather stuck a little but nothing else. As she pulled the one slab of leather off her pinkie finger, they all looked down. There lay a small, folded square of paper, perfectly preserved.

Carefully, Ashley unfolded the paper.

As she unfolded it a third time, she cried out, "I can't believe it! It's part of the treaty! I just knew it would be, but I still can't believe it!"

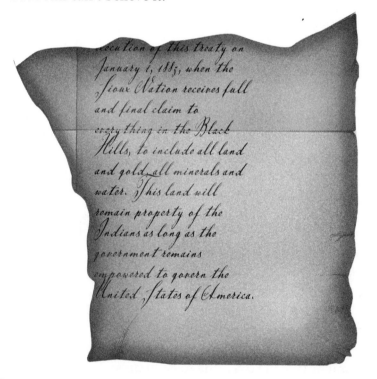

...ecution of this treaty on January 1, 1885, when the Sioux Nation receives full and final claim to everything in the Black Hills, to include all land and gold, all minerals and water. This land will remain property of the Indians as long as the government remains empowered to govern the United States of America.

The small group cheered, and then Elijah spoke.

"You looked deep into the general's eyes, Ashley," he said, "just like he's been telling us to for over a hundred years."

"Quick, Dad, the photocopy of the treaty," Ashley prompted.

"A step ahead of you this time," her father said, pulling a copy from his back pocket. He unfolded it and put it next to the piece Ashley had just uncovered.

She pushed it beneath Jones's piece on the right side, and it fit perfectly. It also lined up just right with Jim Red Feather's piece. Ashley ran her hand across the final line on the copy where it was to meet Crook's piece. "It picks up here."

She started reading Robert Jones's part of the treaty.

Ashley adjusted the bottom piece to pick up on Crook's paper when Jones's left off.

Tears appeared in Elijah Crook's eyes.

"I can't believe this," he said. "We would have given the land back to the Native Americans. My great-great-grandpa wanted to do the right thing, but it just didn't happen. I don't know what to say. I am so shocked, so proud, and so . . . I don't know what else to say."

They all looked at the treaty, and Mr. Arlington shook his head in amazement.

"Simply incredible," he said. "Every clue to this was within the borders of South Dakota, and they've been here for more than a hundred years."

Adam offered to help Elijah put the picture together again. They tucked the burlap back in behind the frame, and Elijah put the screws back into the case.

On this 1st day of January, 18__, the government of the United States of America and all American Indians agree to the terms and conditions of this treaty, which is binding here in this form, and will be formalized within the following two days. This treaty finalizes all arrangements to the ultimate resolution of gold and land rights to the Black Hills in the United States of America. As of this day, until a time 11 years from now on the first day of January, 188_, when the Sioux Nation is to assume full control of the Black Hills. The U.S. government assumes all land rights to the Black Hills. As of January 1, 188_, no white man shall be allowed in the Black Hills. All rail lines must be withdrawn by the U.S. government, and all roads will be left to the Indians to do what they wish as they see fit.

Until the 1st day of January, 188_, no white man is to be harassed or troubled by Indians. All mining activity can continue endlessly until 11 years from this day of January, 187_, until the execution of this treaty on January 1, 188_, when the Sioux Nation receives full and final claim to everything in the Black Hills, to include all land and gold, all minerals and water. This land will remain property of the Indians as long as the government remains empowered to govern the United States of America.

General George Crook

Captain William Grattan

Chon-gah-ma-he-to-hans-ka

Wah-ke-ke-yan-guh-tah

Mar-to-ka-in-yan-ke

Official Document of the government of the United States of America. Contents are said to be binding for the United States of America, all of its people, and the U.S. government

"It doesn't even look like it was ever touched," Ashley said when Mr. Crook held the picture up. He smiled and took the picture back in the room, hanging it in the same spot.

"Oh, if only the general could talk," he said.

"I think in a lot of ways," Adam said, "he already has."

The Puzzle Completed

Late that afternoon, the family sat at a roadside diner outside of Mobridge, on Lake Oahe, enjoying the view and some icy lemonade. They'd said goodbye to Elijah Crook a couple of hours earlier, taking a different route back to the campground. He'd entrusted his piece of the treaty to them for now, and they'd all agreed to be in touch over the next few days.

"You know what we need to do?" Anne Arlington asked her family. "We need to call Jim Red Feather and let him know what's going on."

"Good point, Anne," her husband agreed. "Let's finish up, and we can go call the hospital right now."

Outside at a pay phone, Mr. Arlington dialed the hospital in Rapid City. The switchboard operator told him that Jim Red Feather had been moved to his own room, and when she transferred the call, Ted answered the phone. Jim was doing well but staying in the hospital to rest and be monitored.

"We're heading back from Aberdeen right now," Mr. Arlington told Ted. "We'd sure like to see you and Jim and fill you in on what we've found, if Jim's feeling up to it."

"Oh, I think Dad would love it," Ted said. Mr. Arlington could hear Jim in the background, and it sounded like he was answering questions from a doctor or a nurse.

Ted suggested they come by the hospital the next morning, and after a few moments of friendly chat, Mr. Arlington hung up the phone.

As the Arlingtons prepared for bed in the motor home that night, Ashley picked up her Crazy Horse book and read another chapter before shutting off a small camping lantern and calling it a night. Her dreams took her to the prairies of South Dakota more than a hundred years ago, and when she woke up the next morning, she wished she could go back in time if even for just a precious moment. While she would never feel the wind run through her hair as she hunted buffalo with the legendary Crazy Horse, she felt, at least in some small way, that she could understand some of the pain his people had endured.

Mrs. Arlington called the hospital the following morning to confirm their visit. She was surprised to hear Jim Red Feather answer the phone.

"How are you feeling, Jim?" she asked, concerned.

"I have been better," Jim answered. "But my condition has improved from a few days ago, I can tell you that much. I appreciate the flowers you sent too."

He explained what had happened with the heart attack.

"I went out to my truck to drive to meet you over at Hot Springs, and when I got behind the wheel, I felt like someone had hit me in the chest with a battering ram," Jim said. "I went back inside and called Ted. After that, I cannot remember much of anything until I woke up here."

"We're all just glad you pulled through it," she said. "We were thinking about you when we went to Aberdeen."

"What was in Aberdeen? Did you go to Storybook Land?" Jim asked, in reference to a theme park in Aberdeen.

"No, we were pretty much consumed with figuring out this whole thing about the treaty," Mrs. Arlington said.

"Ted mentioned you had called," Jim said. "We are looking forward to seeing you. Did you find out anything?"

"Sure did," Mrs. Arlington replied. "We'll fill you in at the hospital."

The family took turns getting cleaned up at the motor home. Mr. Arlington showered first and then started a cooking fire and got breakfast going. The family had bacon, eggs, and toast under the awning, with the mosquito netting folded up out of the way since the bugs weren't bad in the cool of the early morning.

"I hate to say it, but wouldn't you call bacon and eggs heart attack food?" Adam said, shoving a forkful into his mouth.

"Adam!" Ashley chided her brother. "Is this really a good time to joke about heart attacks?"

Their father couldn't help but smile. "We know that Jim's out of the woods now, and it's good to lighten up sometimes, don't you think, Ash?"

"Yeah, too bad Adam's sense of humor's so lame," Ashley said, grabbing a piece of her brother's toast and taking a big bite out of it.

"Yum," she said, setting the toast—minus a bite—back down on Adam's plate.

Their mother smiled with a tolerant air. "Present moment aside, Dad and I have been really proud of you both this trip. We've encountered a lot of new things, and we're dealing with some sensitive issues—you've both handled yourselves just as we'd have hoped," she said, smiling.

"Mom and I have both been learning a lot this trip," their father said, putting an arm around his wife. "Any thoughts on what you two will take away from this experience?"

Adam put down his fork and heaved an exaggerated sigh. "I knew this was coming," he said. "Just when you sit down to enjoy a nice meal, or put on some tunes, or get to the good part in your book—BAM. They hit you with the life lesson business," he said, shaking his head.

Everyone shared a laugh. "Well, why don't you start, smarty," his mother prompted.

Adam turned serious and focused on the question. "Okay, well, this is going to sound too simple, but I've really learned that getting along with people seems to be mostly about respect."

"Go on," his father urged.

"Well, relationships between the white settlers and the Indians can't be boiled down to one thing, I know. But it seems like if there'd been more respect for how the American Indians had always lived, everything would be different now. There wouldn't be this kind of lingering mistrust, I guess."

Mrs. Arlington nodded. "We see over and over again in history how people lash out at what they fear—and we see again and again that that's not a productive way to handle our fear of things that are different."

Mr. Arlington put a hand on Ashley's shoulder. "How about you, honey?" he asked. "Anything you want to add?"

"Well, I think the biggest thing I've learned is that you have to be patient," Ashley said. "There were times when we really could have pushed it, like with Mr. Red Feather in the parking lot—but that would've ended up costing us time in the long run."

"Yes, or we might have alienated him and then not been able to be of help," Mrs. Arlington added.

"Yeah—it's just that when he was standing there at the gas station and told us the paper meant something to him, I was just dying for any little bit of information he could give us. I wanted just one thing to go on, but he wanted us to wait. And none of us said anything. We just waited. And then we ended up sharing a special time with his family and hearing the story about Wounded Knee. And then everything started to mean so much more."

"So your impatience didn't get you anywhere?" Mr. Arlington asked.

"It got me nowhere fast," Ashley said, "as usual."

"Okay, you two," their mother said. "How do you use what you've learned from this trip when we get back home?"

"That's easy for me," Ashley said. "I've always battled being patient enough. I can use it with my friends especially, hearing them out before I add my thoughts. I can use it in basketball too, making sure I don't always rush, rush, rush when there is obviously something to be gained by waiting just a second."

"And you, Adam?" Mrs. Arlington asked.

"I just have to be respectful of people—I know I want people to respect me too and hear me out when I have something to say that might be different from what they're thinking. I knew that already, but sometimes I don't act the way I should," he said.

"Well, luckily we are given the opportunity to learn the same lessons again and again," his mother pointed out.

"At least we have something to think about if there's ever some sort of next time," Mr. Arlington said.

They all looked at each other and broke out laughing.

"A next time?" Mrs. Arlington cried, grabbing her husband and playfully ruffling his graying hair. "What do you mean next time? The next time we come to South Dakota, we're going to have our own treaty, one that thoroughly spells out the way we are going to do nothing but relax every day of our vacation!"

A half-hour later, the Arlingtons were heading northeast to Rapid City. Ashley carried the photocopies of the treaty into the hospital while her mother had the originals in the transparent, airtight container. Ted Red Feather was in his father's room as the Arlingtons arrived, and so was Leonard Jumping Bear.

Jim Red Feather had as much color in his face as when the Arlingtons spent time with him at Wounded Knee, so they assumed he was well on the road to recovery. He sat up in his bed and pushed aside a table that had a meal on it.

"Okay, who will fill me in?" Jim asked with a smile.

Ashley launched right in, excited about what they'd found. "You were right when you said that this treaty could have changed the face of America," she said. "Not to mention the face of Mount Rushmore—it might've had Custer on it. Or Crazy Horse and Sitting Bull," she added with a wide grin.

Ashley pulled out the photocopies of the four pieces together, and passed them out to the small group. She then read the entire treaty from start to finish. Adam expected a cheer or some sort of reaction. However, while there was a look of disbelief among everyone in the room who was hearing the news for the first time, no one said a word.

"So, what do you think, Mr. Red Feather?" Ashley asked after a moment.

Everyone in the room could see the emotion in Jim's eyes.

"I cannot believe you put it all together," he said softly. "I still have no reason to believe the government would ever have honored this treaty more than any of the others. That said, it is still a relief to finally have this piece of history accounted for. Just thinking about the possibilities of what could have happened had the treaty become law is exciting."

"How did you get all the pieces?" Leonard asked. "You visited Robert Jones in Hot Springs, right?"

"We did," Ashley said. She then recounted the story, picking it up from the morning after they got the second piece of the treaty at Ted's farm. Ashley talked about how Robert Jones had opened the safe-deposit box.

"That's incredible," Ted said, shaking his head in disbelief. "I really didn't have much faith that anything would come of this. I thought that night at my place was the end of it; I really did."

After updating everyone in the room on Robert Jones's plans to return to his heritage and also help out Native Americans with several innovative banking programs, Ashley explained the connection to General Crook. She told them how helpful Elijah Crook had been.

"From everything I've heard about him," Ted said, "he seems to be a decent man."

For the next half an hour or so, everyone talked about the treaty. Jim, Ted, and Leonard spoke of how things might be different today. There was some serious emotion as they talked about how the Black Hills would still be a religious area, about how buffalo might roam as far as the eye could see, and how the younger generations of Sioux would have had a better opportunity to hold on to their culture. Mostly, they talked about what the Sioux could have done had they regained control of the Black Hills. And, of course, they spoke of Crazy Horse.

"Crazy Horse would've never had to head down to Fort Robinson in 1877," Leonard said. "He would have led the Indians back into the Black Hills into a new era of prosperity."

They talked about Custer as well.

"Long Hair probably wishes this treaty had never been torn up," Ted said with a smile, referring to Custer, whose

Little Bighorn battle might never have taken place had the treaty stood.

"Instead of Custer State Park, it would be Sitting Bull State Park—just for our people," Leonard added. "No offense," he added, smiling a little awkwardly at the Arlingtons.

"Really, what I would rather have seen is that it be for white people too, to visit in the same way they visit Mount Rushmore today," Jim said. "They could have learned our culture, and they would respect it more. Some might even have become attached to the Sioux ways.

"I would like to see everyone, all kinds of people, enjoy this document," Jim Red Feather said, picking up his photocopy of the treaty once again. "This document has no legal meaning of course. But it does say something important about an effort by the white man to bridge the gap with our people, even though it was unsuccessful. I think people would enjoy this."

"I know they would," Adam said eagerly. "It's so cool!"

Jim and Ted chuckled at Adam's enthusiasm.

"Any idea what we should do with the original pieces?" Jim asked, setting his copy of the treaty aside.

"How about showing them at the Crazy Horse Monument?" Ashley suggested.

Jim Red Feather nodded slowly.

"I can see that happening," Ted said.

Leonard started to smile, caught up in a scene in his mind. "It could be near the gift shop where the smaller scale Crazy Horse sculpture—the one of how the finished monument will look—where that's standing. This treaty all comes back to Crazy Horse," he said. "Maybe just displaying this treaty at the monument might help it get finished one day. Might charge people up as it has us."

Jim nodded, looking around at the small group. "I am charged up; I can tell you that," he said enthusiastically. "And I am getting tired of wearing this hospital-issue nightgown," he added, fingering the pale cotton gown. "Ted—when will you get me out of here?"

Mitaku Oyasin

The Arlingtons spent the afternoon enjoying Wind Cave National Park near where their motor home was parked. Hiking through miles of lush woods and grassland, they saw bison, deer, and antelope. Late in the day, they took a tour of Wind Cave and learned that it's the sixth largest cave in the world. Down below ground, the guide pointed out fantastic features formed by deposits in the cave—features with descriptive names like boxwood, popcorn, and frostwork.

"This has really been our first true 'vacation' day this trip," Adam pointed out when they returned to their motor home that evening.

"I know, we've been too hot on the treaty trail to do the things we'd planned on doing here," Ashley agreed.

Their father smiled as he set the picnic table for dinner. "But if I were a gambling man, I'd bet you wouldn't trade this experience for any vacation in the world," he said.

"No way," Ashley said. "This has really been amazing—

it's the kind of thing we could have missed out on by inches, you know what I mean?"

"Yeah—like if you'd picked out a different book in the stack that day," Adam pointed out.

The family ate buffalo burgers cooked on the grill, along with some salads they'd bought at the store, and then called it an early night. For the first time since she opened the Crazy Horse book, Ashley found herself able to relax. She read a hundred pages that night before falling into a deep, peaceful sleep.

The next day, the family visited the capital city of Pierre. Outside the city, they stopped at a buffalo ranch. Ashley was amazed by herds the likes of which she'd only seen before in movies. And Adam tried to count all the prairie dogs in sight, but they seemed to tease him by popping in and out of their holes.

They drove along miles of grassland, occasionally spotting a pronghorn running as fast as the car. They drove to the Fort Manual Trading Post where Sacajawea, the Shoshone Indian woman guide for Lewis and Clark, is said to be buried, before driving home to the campground at Wind Cave.

The cell phone was ringing as Mrs. Arlington stepped up into the motor home, and she quickly grabbed it. It was Jim Red Feather, inviting them to a gathering at the Crazy Horse Monument the next afternoon.

"This'll be great," Mrs. Arlington said after hanging up and filling in her family. "Ted and Stephanie, Robin and Denise, Leonard Jumping Bear—everybody'll be there for a big late-afternoon chow-down and storytelling in the picnic area. Also, Jim has invited Elijah Crook and his family too. And Robert Jones."

"Yeah, yeah, that's great. But did he talk about the most important thing?" Adam asked.

His mother looked concerned. "You mean the treaty?"

"No—did he say what they're having for dinner?"

The next morning was as gorgeous as it had been any day during the vacation. The cool morning air seemed fresher, and the sun seemed even brighter. The Arlingtons decided to get an early start and spend the morning mountain-biking in the Black Hills National Forest.

Biking through miles of single-track, Adam and Ashley were thrilled by the piney smell of the evergreens and the challenging trails.

"Did you know that we're in the midst of what's been called a 'sea of pine trees'—the trees are so thick the whole landscape looks black from a distance," Ashley explained to her brother.

Adam grinned. "Oh, I get it: the Black Hills. Cool."

After three hours of riding, the four loaded their bikes back onto the racks on the SUV and headed back to camp to get cleaned up for the afternoon's event.

Adam and Ashley dressed nicely—no jeans, tennis shoes or T-shirts—very respectfully for the occasion. Ashley, who rarely wore a dress, had on a green cornsilk skirt that reached all the way down to the top of the tan boots she was wearing. Her light green, button-up top went well with it, and she had a sweater draped around her neck. Adam wore a white shirt and black cotton pants and carried a black sweater.

They arrived at Crazy Horse Monument right on time, and it looked like the other guests had been eager to gather too. The Arlingtons greeted Jim, who was dressed in a beautiful beaded shirt, and Robin and Denise, who were wearing traditional buckskin dresses.

"Wow," Ashley said, eyeing the girls' beaded clothing. "Those are a lot prettier than half the dresses at our prom last year."

"Thank you," the girls said shyly before walking away to join their relatives.

Leonard Jumping Bear, Ted and Stephanie, Jim's daughter, Gail, whom the Arlingtons hadn't met yet, and Robin and Denise all started dancing to the beat of a drum.

"I still have to sit the dancing out for a while," Jim said to the Arlingtons. But he chanted along with the others while they danced. Elijah Crook and his family came over, and they exchanged greetings with the Arlingtons, and then Robert Jones and his family showed up.

"We are so glad you are here," Leonard Jumping Bear said as he left the dance ring and embraced Jones.

"We wouldn't miss it," Jones said to him. He then turned to Ashley. "Well, you did it, didn't you?"

"We all did it, Mr. Jones," Ashley said with a smile.

The drumbeat stopped then, and Jim greeted everyone. "Please, gather around, everybody," he called. As he spoke, copies of the treaty were passed around. They were like the ones Ashley made, only the paper was thicker, rough on the edges and yellowish—as though it had been aged, just like the treaty.

"We'll have to save these," Adam whispered to his mother and father.

"This treaty," Jim continued, "is a piece of history. And it could have made a difference to our people; the fact is, it was never enacted. But I think we have the unique opportunity to accept this as part of the healing process. And believe me, I know about the healing process," he said, tapping a finger on his chest.

There was a collective chuckle as Jim joked about his recovery from the heart attack.

"So, thanks to everyone for being here," Jim said. "And thanks to Elijah Crook for coming—I think we can all agree that his great-great-grandfather was an honorable man."

Elijah Crook looked down at his feet. He was proud of his ancestor, but to have Jim appreciate the general was very moving.

"And thanks especially to the Arlingtons, who made this possible. For it is this family from this nation's capital in Washington, D.C., who gave up their vacation to help give us this treaty. We welcome them to the Paha Sapa where they are always welcome at my family's home."

The small gathering clapped warmly and everyone smiled. "Speech, speech!" Leonard Jumping Bear hollered playfully.

The Arlingtons laughed, and after a moment of hesitation, Ashley spoke up. "You know, I never had any idea how this would turn out when the first piece of the treaty fell out of the book I bought up here at the gift shop. But it's better than I could have hoped," she said, looking around at her new friends. She looked at her mother as if to ask permission to go on, or to seek encouragement. Everyone was smiling at her, expectant.

"I guess what I know now is that you don't undo more than a century of hurt and pain with the flip of a switch or with a few little scraps of paper," Ashley said. "I can't really talk about what should have happened or what might have happened—but it seems like the fact that this treaty never became law isn't what matters today. What matters is that all of us are together, right? Respecting each other and enjoying the new friendships we've made with each other.

"I'm sorry we have to leave South Dakota so soon," she went on. "But I'll tell my friends back home about what we've seen here. I'll tell them, 'Come to the Black Hills, and tread lightly on this ground because it is sacred to my Sioux brothers and sisters.'"

Ashley smiled awkwardly. "That sounds a bit strange," she said. "But I know how much we've appreciated being treated like family here."

"Mitaku Oyasin," Jim interjected, smiling.

"Mitaku Oyasin," Ashley repeated. "Who knows, but I think that if that rock were to soften today, Crazy Horse would smile down on this gathering."

A big meal followed, and everyone cheered when Jim announced plans were underway to put the treaty on display in the Crazy Horse Monument visitors' center. The Arlingtons couldn't have imagined a more satisfying outcome to their whole vacation experience. So it was a tired, happy family that headed back to the motor home that night after saying good-bye to their new friends.

There was a lot of packing and cleaning to be done starting the next morning—it was time the family was heading home.

As Adam logged onto his computer that night and his parents played cards in the back of the motor home, Ashley sat down outside, tucked her legs under the Indian quilt, and clicked on the camping lamp.

She opened her Crazy Horse book. But this time, instead of something slipping out of the book and onto her lap, she fell deep into the book, staying up past midnight to finish it.

Ashley was sad to read the end, as Crazy Horse died from a stab wound after he had surrendered for the good of his people at Fort Robinson.

"Tell the people," the dying Crazy Horse told his father, "it is no use to depend on me anymore now."

Ashley set the book on her lap and leaned back in her lawn chair. Her eyes swept the flecked blackness just as a shooting star zipped across the sky. She suddenly remembered what Jim had said—that some believe the great leaders could be seen in the stars.

"Just a coincidence," she told herself. But the warm feeling Ashley Arlington suddenly felt on the chilly night made her smile up at the stars. "We are still depending on you, Crazy Horse," she whispered.

South Dakota

Fun
Fact
Files

South Dakota

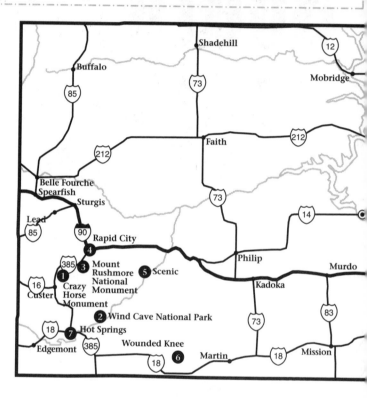

The Arlingtons' Route

1. Crazy Horse Monument
2. Wind Cave National Monument
3. Mount Rushmore National Monument
4. Rapid City
5. Scenic
6. Wounded Knee
7. Hot Springs
8. Aberdeen
9. Pierre
10. Crazy Horse Monument

Names and Symbols

Origin of Name:

When Dakota territory was created in 1861, it was named for the Dakota tribe. *Dakota* is a Sioux word meaning "friends" or "allies."

Nicknames:

Mount Rushmore State, Sunshine State, Coyote State

South Dakota was long known as the Sunshine State because it's state motto, which appeared on the state flag, was "Sunshine State." In 1980 the motto, flag, and nickname were changed to be the Mount Rushmore State. The nickname Coyote State was inspired by a swift horse.

Motto:

"Under God the People Rule"

State Symbols:

flower—pasque flower
tree—Black Hills spruce
stones—rose quartz and fairburn agate
bird—ring-necked pheasant
animal—coyote
fish—walleye

Geography

Location:

Northern Great Plains

Borders:

North Dakota (north)
Minnesota and Iowa (east)
Nebraska (south)
Wyoming (west)

Area:

77,122 square miles (16th largest state)

Highest Elevation:

Harney Peak, Pennington County (7,242 feet)

Lowest Elevation:

Big Stone Lake, Roberts County (966 feet)

Nature

National Parks and Monuments:

Badlands National Park
Jewel Cave National Monument
Mount Rushmore National Memorial
Wind Cave National Park

National Forests:

Black Hills National Forest
Custer National Forest

Weather

Located far from the sea, South Dakota enjoys a continental climate, with hot summers and cold winters made more bitter by winds that sweep across the treeless plains. South Dakota has long been known as the Blizzard State for its winter storms. Rainfall is light, with the more arid areas in western South Dakota, as is evidenced by the Badlands.

People and Cities

Population:

738, 000 (1998 census)
696,000 (1990 census)

Capital:

Pierre

Ten Largest Cities (as of 1998):

Sioux Falls (113,223)
Rapid City (57,642)
Aberdeen (25,088)
Watertown (19,619)
Brookings (17,413)
Mitchell (14,191)
Yankton (13,969)
Pierre (13,422)
Huron (12,428)
Vermillon (10,521)

Counties:

67 (64 county governments)

Major Industries

Agriculture:

South Dakota leads the nation in production of hay and oats; it ranks second in production of rye, flaxseed, and sunflower seeds. Corn, wheat, soybeans, and hay are the chief cash crops.

Richest farmland is east of the Missouri River; the "West River" country is more arid and is largely used for grazing cattle and sheep.

Manufacturing:

Meat packing and food processing are the state's major industries.

Mining:

South Dakota's most important mineral is gold. Berylium, betonite, granite, silver, uranium, stone, sand, gravel, and cement are also important to the economy.

The nation's leading gold-mining center is the Homestake Mine in the Black Hills.

Tourism:

Many visitors travel through South Dakota enroute to western states.

State tourist attractions include the Black Hills, Mount Rushmore, the Badlands, and Wall Drug.

History

Native Americans:

In 1804 the region was inhabited by the agricultural Arikara and the nomadic Sioux (Dakota) Indians. By the 1830s the Sioux had driven the Arikara away and were bracing for an assault by white explorers and settlers. War broke out when whites invaded the sacred Black Hills in search of gold. Sitting Bull, Crazy Horse, and Gall were among the famous Sioux warriors who fought the U.S. Army in present South Dakota and neighboring areas. Many Native Americans were killed or confined to reservations. Hope was renewed by a new "Ghost Dance" religion, but was dashed with Sitting Bull's death in 1890 and the subsequent Wounded Knee Massacre.

Native Americans have increasingly moved to the cities. Today, almost one third of the region west of the Missouri River belongs to Native Americans. Most of them live on reservations such as Rosebud, Pine Ridge, Cheyenne River, and Standing Rock. The last of the Plains Indians were the focus of the popular movie *Dances with Wolves,* which was filmed in South Dakota.

Exploration and Settlement:

Louis-Joseph and François Verendrye came from France in 1743 to explore the area in search of a route to the Pacific. After the United States made the vast Louisiana Purchase, Lewis and Clark were commissioned to follow the Missouri River across the Dakotas in 1804–6. In 1817 the fur trade inspired the founding of Fort Pierre, the first permanent settlement. The first Missouri River steamboat reached the fort in 1831. In 1873 the railroad arrived. Gold was discovered in the Black Hills the following year.

Territory:

organized as Dakota Territory (included North and South Dakota, eastern Wyoming, and eastern Montana) on March 2, 1861

Statehood:

entered the union on November 2, 1889, along with North Dakota (39th/40th state)

Check It Out

For more information about the historical people and places in this book, check out the following books and web sites:

South Dakota

Web site: http://www.state.sd.us/

Badlands National Park

Web site: http://www.nps.gov/badl/exp/frame-index.htm

Crazy Horse

Book: St. George, Judith S. *Crazy Horse.* New York: Putnam, 1994.

Web site: http://www.crazyhorse.org/

Custer State Park

Web sites:
http://www.state.sd.us/sdparks/custer/custer.htm

http://www.pbs.org/weta/thewest/wpages/wpgs400/w4custer.htm

General George Crook

Web site: http://www.pbs.org/weta/thewest/wpages/wpgs400/w4crook.htm

Ghost Dance Story

Web site: http://www.msnbc.com/onair/msnbc/
TimeandAgain/archive/wknee/ghost.asp?cp1=1

Lakota/Sioux Indians

Books: Driving, Virginia. *The Sioux : A First Americans Book.* Illustrated by Ronald Himler. New York: Holiday House, 1993.

Dominic, Gloria. *Brave Bear and the Ghosts: A Sioux Legend.* Illustrated by Charles Reasoner. Vero Beach, Fla.: Rourke Corp., 1998.

Left Hand Bull, Jacqueline. *Lakota Hoop Dancer.* Illustrated by Suzanne Haldane. New York: Dutton Books, 1999.

Nicholson, Robert. *The Sioux.* Broomall, Pa.: Chelsea House Publishing, 1994.

Web sites:

http://blackhills-info.com/lakota_sioux/index.htm

http://maple.lemoyne.edu/~bucko/lakota.html

Mount Rushmore

Book: Doherty, Craig A. and Katherine M. *Mount Rushmore: Building America.* Edited by Bruce Glassman. Boulder, Colo.: Blackbirch, 1995.

Web sites: http://www.nps.gov/moru/

http://www.travelsd.com/rushmore/

Wounded Knee

Books: O'Neill, Laurie A. *Wounded Knee: The Death of a Dream.* Brookfield, Conn.: Millbrook Press, 1994.

Stein, Richard Conrad. *The Story of Wounded Knee.* Danbury, Conn.: Children's Press, 1989

Web site: http://www.ibiscom.com/knee.htm

Also Available . . .

Message in MONTANA

0-8010-4454-5
$5.99

✖ When Adam Arlington forgets to pack games for the family's trip to Montana, the Arlingtons improvise and find a used "game" at a local store. The family soon discovers that what they believed to be merely a beat-up game is actually the first step in an exciting new quest. Unsure what to expect, the family follows the cryptic clues from city to city, learning about the Lewis & Clark expedition along the way. Finally they find themselves back almost where they bagan, uncovering a new page in Lewis and Clark history.

Watch for more books in the X-Country Adventures series

Ashley and Adam Arlington have a knack for uncovering mysteries wherever they go—even while on vacation in the various states. Each book in this series presents a new puzzle for the Arlington siblings to solve.

0-8010-4453-7 $5.99

Crime in a COLORADO Cave

✖ While visiting Cave of the Winds in Colorado, Ashley and Adam Arlington are caught up in the task of catching the thieves who steal a display of costly crystals from the cave's visitor center. The siblings must use their observational skills and critical thinking to help the police officer on the case put the pieces together and recover the stolen crystals.

Adventure in WYOMING

0-8010-4452-9 $5.99

✖ When a family friend mysteriously disappears just hours after having served as their climbing guide, the Arlingtons set out to help in any way they can. Their sleuthing leads to more adventure than they bargained for, though, as they trek across the state on a clue-gathering mission that leads them to beautiful Yellowstone National Park.

Sports writer and newspaper editor **Bob Schaller** has won several awards for his journalistic excellence. Now a full-time writer, he is the author of The Olympic Dream and Spirit series, which covers athletes such as Mary Lou Retton, Dan O'Brien, Andre Agassi, and Dominique Moceanu. Schaller is also writing a biography of U.S. Olympic swimmer Amy Van Dyken. He lives in Colorado Springs, Colorado.